"H.B. Bent [...] that rustler?" asked Erv.

"No, ma'am."

"I didn't want to believe you were some kind of hardened killer, and me, well, you know."

"Holding hands with one?" I asked.

"I can't decide whether you're some kind of butterfly cowboy that rides around the country breaking girls' hearts or what."

"Butterfly cowboy? What the hell is that?" I frowned at her as we went hand-swinging along under the spray of stars.

"Oh, someone that roams around kissing girls like a damn butterfly goes from flower to flower."

"I'm not one of those." Why was I even in this conversation with Erv? I needed to go saddle my cow pony and trail those two drunks and have it out with them.

"A girl hates to be trifled with."

"Erv, I've never trifled with you!"

"You damn sure did! That day you rode up and kissed me, you trifled with me!"

I spun her around and kissed her. This time I kissed her like I meant it, with her bent over in my arms. I stood her up and felt her upper arms tremble under my hands.

"That's trifling," I said sharply. . . .

Books by Dusty Richards

From Hell to Breakfast*
Noble's Way

*Published by POCKET BOOKS

FROM HELL TO BREAKFAST

DUSTY RICHARDS

POCKET BOOKS

New York   London   Toronto   Sydney   Tokyo   Singapore

An *Original* Publication of POCKET BOOKS

POCKET BOOKS, a division of Simon & Schuster Inc.
1230 Avenue of the Americas, New York, NY 10020

ISBN: 0-671-87241-9

First Pocket Books printing April 1994

10 9 8 7 6 5 4 3 2 1

POCKET and colophon are registered trademarks of
Simon & Schuster Inc.

Cover art by Tim Tanner

Printed in the U.S.A.

Dedication

This book is dedicated to an old pard and lots of helpers. If it hadn't been for Gene Miller, I'd never really know Horseafucious Bentley. Gene and I rode hundreds of miles horseback across Arizona, danced with lots of gals in schoolhouses and in bars. We skipped school and chased mustangs, cowboyed, tube-floated rivers, and rodeoed. But he was the one who awoke the writer in me with a letter: *"Why ain't you written that Western book?"*

I owe a lot to my wife, Pat, who encourages me. To the great Western writer Fred Bean, who rode roughshod over me, I owe a debt. And I give my thanks to all my compadres in the Western Writers of America who kept the faith. Last but not least, my Stetson's off to my editor, Doug Grad, who knew where this book was stashed away. *Gracias, amigos.*

FROM
HELL
TO
BREAKFAST

Mr. Hainey up on the North Cut promised me a fall roundup job. I'd spent all summer cutting alfalfa hay down on the Salt River near Phoenix. My butt was callused from riding an iron seat mower, and my brain was dulled by the all-day clack-clack of the cutter bar. Saturday evening I collected my wages from John Daniel and went to saddle my cow pony, Short, to head up for the North Cut.

Short had fattened all summer on the Daniels' fodder. His brown hide was slick as a mole. As usual, the bay gelding acted a little snorty when I saddled him. I kept an eye on his heels, because he occasionally cow-kicked at me during the saddling process. A man learned a horse's bad habits and those he couldn't break—he made mental notes about how to avoid them. Short had a passel of shortcomings.

1

"H.B., are you coming by the house to say good-bye?" Mr. Daniel asked.

"Sure thing, sir," I said, reaching under Short's belly for the back cinch. When I drew it up, the cow pony gave me a mean look, but Short hated all human beings, no matter what they did around him.

"I'm sure going to miss you around here," Mr. Daniel said, busy forking hay over to his draft horses. I silently agreed. He'd miss me feeding them horses, doing all his dang chores, and pitching hay from sunup till sundown, things he'd have to start doing himself.

"I may need work again sometime," I said, tying my bedroll on and booting Short hard in the belly as he telegraphed drawing up his left hind foot for a sneaky kick at me.

"If you need work next hay session, I'd sure rehire you, H.B.," Mr. Daniel said, hanging over the corral fence and looking my outfit over. "That ol' pony of yours sure got snuffy standing around in these corrals all summer, ain't he?"

"Short? Oh, he's a little snorty-acting now, but he'll be fine when I swing a leg over his back."

"I had a horse like that once. Acted just like him. I sold that rascal first chance I got."

"I like a horse with a little spunk," I said defensively. Near forty, Mr. Daniel was getting up in years, so he didn't want to mess with a real spirited horse.

I led Short across the open yard toward the white-washed house with the trim picket fence. At the gate I picked up my war bag full of personal things and tied it on the saddle horn, along with my latest issue of the *Police Gazette,* which I stuffed in my saddlebags.

When I stuck my boot toe in the stirrup, Short's nostrils flared and he snorted. Then he set his pin ears flat on his head, squinted his little pig eyes, and when I swung up, all hell broke loose out in front of the Daniel house.

That crazy pony, with his head between his knees, left out bucking. The second jump—he busted flat a large section of picket fence and charged into the yard. With my left hand pulling leather, my right hand jerking his jaw, and both of my toes out of the stirrups, we were scattering Mrs. Daniel's pullets in a cloud of squawking feathers. That didn't cover the damage to her flowers Short's hooves were shredding with every lunge he made.

"Whoa, you idiot!" I screamed, wondering when Short would quit his bucking.

Mrs. Daniel burst out on the porch armed with a broom to attack this demon in her flowers. I briefly saw her red face, but for the most part, I was trying to stay in the saddle through all of Short's wild gyrations. At the moment, I'd have sold Short cheap to the soap factory. But more than anything else I dreaded hitting the ground, or worse—facing Mrs. Daniel's fury. The grasshopper under me was still bucking furious and grunting like a mad hog with every jump. Short laid down ten more feet of picket fence leaving the yard, crow-hopping his heart away.

Short and I left the Daniels' ranch, her hens scared out of a month's lay, the flower beds stomped, and over a month's wages in damages to Mrs. Daniel's precious white picket fence.

Short finally broke into a lope. Mrs. Daniel's ringing threats grew more distant. I reached back and made sure my bedroll was still tied on. The saddlebags were still buckled down, and even the war bag was there. I whipped old Short with the reins, and I was headed for the fall roundup on the North Cut at a hard gallop.

I'd intended to leave the Daniels without any ill feelings and I regretted the damages, but it damn sure wasn't my fault. Short was a worthless ornery horse to own, 'cept he was all the horse I could afford to own on the wages I earned.

After three days riding and two nights camped out with the coyotes, I drew up Short to stop and study Linter's Store. The unpainted structure looked inviting in the valley. There were other riders there at the crossroads store—I saw them standing around their horses. With the rich smell of the piñon and juniper in my nose and the blue-green line of the towering Mogollon Rim to the north, I felt certain I'd be at Mr. Hainey's ranch by dark. The cool mountain wind on my face was a relief after the broiling summer of haying in the Salt River Valley.

When I rode up to Linter's Store, three cowboys were drinking sarsaparilla from brown bottles over by the set of corrals. They wore long-tail linen dusters and snap-brim cowboys hats. None of them looked my way, so I figured they weren't interested in talking. I dismounted and tied Short to the hitch rail. Then I glanced again in their direction, but they were behind their horses and didn't act at all friendly. Their attitude sure made me wonder. A stranger rides up in a new place and usually the ranch hands will rush over and shake his hand. Folks in the North Cut must not be that all-fired friendly.

I hitched up my chaps and jeans and started inside Linter's Store. The faded sign on the false front told me the name of the place; early that morning a teamster on the road had given me directions. Mr. Hainey lived just twelve miles north. I wanted to buy a few personal things before I rode up and presented myself to the new boss. I'd met Mr. Hainey in Phoenix when I hauled in a load of alfalfa and he'd been there at the livery. I certainly hoped he hadn't forgotten his job offer and hired someone else.

The interior of the store smelled of yard goods, that formaldehyde odor that nearly draws your tears up. There was also an aroma of saddle oil, smoked meat, and cigar smoke in the air. The front tables were piled high with folded canvas jeans and a mountain of lace-up work shoes. Kettles and skillets hung down from the rafters. I must have been awestruck by the plentiful merchandise, for I nearly ran into a bear-sized man with a black beard, his arms full of packages.

"Who the hell are you?" he demanded with a frown of complete disapproval at my presence in his way.

"H.B.," I said, wondering if everyone in this crossroads was as cranky as him or as stuck-up as those three punchers outside.

"H.B. what?"

"Bentley." He might have been big, but he sorely needed some lessons in manners. Most folks in Arizona were a damn sight more friendly, or they'd be pushing up daisies in the cemetery. Folks in the West were tolerant, but they sure didn't contend with boar hogs' dispositions in men.

He managed to free a big finger crested with stiff black hair and wave it at me. With a shift of his armload, I expected him to try for his gun.

"I've never heard of you, but you look like worthless saddle trash to me!"

"I beg your pardon?" I damn sure wished I had worn that .31-caliber Colt from my saddlebags. I was ready to talk with my gun. This man wasn't in his right mind talking to me or to anyone like that.

"Listen, we ain't got a place up here for your kind of shiftless tramps. Ranchers around here have had enough cattle stolen, slow-elked, and run to death. You loaf around here very long on this range and you'll find your neck in a noose!"

"For your information, I have a job in this country."

His dark eyes flew open in disbelief. "Working for what outfit?"

"Mr. Hainey. And next time we meet I may just teach you some better manners." I knew my face must be blazing; the skin felt on fire.

"Hainey, huh?"

"Here! Here! You two, there'll be no fighting in my store!" I saw past the big man. The store clerk behind the counter had a sawed-off greener aimed at the two of us. It sobered up a lot of my anger. I stepped aside, and the big man surged on by. He was still mad as a bear with a thorn in his paw.

After he went outside, I advanced on the man with the shotgun. My hands half-raised, I stood before him.

"I didn't come in here looking for trouble."

"I know, but you have to understand that Ewell's very upset. Two men have been killed. He and the other ranchers have lost several head of cattle, and any stranger is a suspect."

I glanced back out the front glass. He and his stuck-up cowboys were getting ready to ride out. Good riddance.

"If they're all as friendly as him and those snooty cowboys outside, they can have this place. Mister, I've come a hundred miles and I badly need a can of peaches to eat here—what's so damn funny?" The man was choked up on something hilarious. I didn't know what was tickling him.

"My name's Linter," he eventually said, putting the scattergun under the counter. "You can call me Carl."

Then he became so consumed again in his own laughter, he was forced to spread his large, unsun-tanned hands on the counter to support himself. "Sorry, H.B.," he finally managed. "Those cowboys you spoke of . . . ain't cowboys at all. Those are his daughters! See, Ewell Rice never had any boys. Those riders are his girls."

"Girls for cowboys?" I gave Carl Linter a look of disbelief. Pretty silly deal; why, I never knew a woman could ride or rope with a man. Rice must have sheep to herd, or maybe milk cows.

"They're the toughest ranch hands in the valley," Carl said flatly.

"They're the snottiest too."

"Don't mess with them," Carl said, going after my peaches. "Those girls can whip most boys in this country that give them any trouble."

"You mean their daddy would do it?"

Carl turned with the can in his hand. "He won't need to. Those gals are tough as any man walking. Why, they've been doing a man's work since they were little."

"How old are they?"

"Stout is the oldest, she's maybe eighteen, Erv is a year younger, and Tate's fifteen or so."

My mouth was watering to open that can of peaches. I'd probably splurge and eat two cans, but one was to start. "That's their names?"

"I told you Rice never had any boys. Those girls are his ranch crew."

"Stranger things have happened. I better get started on my peaches. I can make it to Mr. Hainey's by dark, can't I?"

"Sure can," Carl said. "You know Hainey very well?"

I raised up from opening my jackknife that I intended to use on the can top. "He isn't crazy as Rice, is he?" What if he was? I'd rode a hundred miles for nothing. Why, I'd never last a half day working for a man like Rice. We'd either be fighting or my butt would be fired.

It took Carl a moment or two before he grinned away my fears. "No, he's a great old cowboy."

I gave a loud exhale in relief. "I figured that the first time we met down in Phoenix."

"If Zack Hainey likes you, you're in good company. But you'll still have to put up with Rice and those girls."

I sawed on the can top to open it, already tasting those sweet syrupy peaches. Whiskey's fine and I drink beer with my friends, but a can of sweet peaches is better than a day off to sleep in the bunkhouse.

"Does Hainey and Rice share the same range?"

"Exactly."

The peaches were there. All wadded up in a red-tinged thick syrup. They had my full attention. But I wanted to know one more thing about those so-called cowgirls.

"Do those girls always ride their horses clothespin style?"

"They do, and they ride like Apaches."

Not taking my eye off the contents of the can, I headed for the front porch and some long-awaited pleasure. The sight of those luscious peach halves floating around inside the open lip of the bright can held my complete concentration as I balanced the contents in my right hand, my left hand holding the jackknife to spear them out.

"Carl, I'll be back in a moment to pay you." But when I turned to see if his reaction to my offer was acceptable, my right spur caught on the threshold. I rushed forward to save my balance.

"Watch out!" someone shouted. I tripped and sprawled belly down on the front porch. The jack-knife flew from my grasp to stick in the ground. My precious peaches flung out of the can and under Short's belly in the dust. The action drew a walleyed snort out of him and he flew back, testing the leather reins.

"You're kinda clumsy, ain't yeh?" someone asked in an amused voice standing above me.

I twisted and looked up at one of those cowgirls. I saw she wore men's jeans under a cotton dress, with her long-tailed canvas duster open because she had her hands on her hips. Full-faced, she reminded me of her father.

"Guess it don't make much difference," I said as a couple of hungry brown hens rushed in to attack the scattered peach halves and expertly avoided Short's stomping hooves. "I sure had other plans for them peaches besides chicken feed."

Her hand shot out, and I accepted the pull to my feet. It was hard for a girl's paw, callused, and I knew by her grip she was no house bug. I swear her shoulders were broader than mine, and she was as tall as me when I faced her.

"My name's Stout," she said, looking at me with her steel gray eyes intent, like a man would a stranger.

"H.B.," I said.

"Welcome to North Cut, H.B.," she said, and inspected me from head to toe. "Nothing broke, huh?"

"Not hardly," I said, and touched my hat. "Thanks for the hand up and nice to meet you, ma'am."

"You ever get to the Pecan School House on Saturday night, you can ask me to dance." She gave me a sharp nod and went inside the store.

I studied her back for a long moment. I'd never danced with a cowgirl before, much less a gal belonged to an old man grouchy as Ewell Rice. But I had her permission to dance anyway, and she was not some quiet schoolgirl.

Stout hurried back outside with something her father had no doubt forgotten. For a moment she paused in front of me. She shifted her weight from boot to boot like she couldn't conjure up what she wanted to say to me.

"Both my sisters dance too," she finally offered.

"I'll be looking forward to it."

"Paw said you was pretty gutsy." She nodded her head as if she was thinking on it. "I figure you are too. I hope one thing, H.B., you don't plan to wear them damn spurs to the dance." She leaned her head over a little to inspect them.

"I won't have them on."

"Good, then Saturday night. Oh, you can come by our wagon there on the grounds before sundown; we'll have a basket lunch to share."

"Mighty nice of you to invite me. Your paw won't shoot me?"

Stout blinked her eyes. "No, he likes folks that got some backbone."

"Saturday night at the Pecan School House?"

"Yes." And she was gone with a swish of her duster.

I must have stared after her for a long time as she rode off before I heard Carl asking from the doorway, "H.B., are you ready for another can of peaches?"

I was ready.

⊀ 2 ⊁

The late afternoon sun slanted long shadows on the main road. Short held a long running walk as we skirted the course of the North Cut. No one called the North Cut a river or a creek; it headwatered up high in the Mogollon at a place called Spider. Starting as a mountain stream, it became a river with sandbars and cottonwoods that rushed through this portion headed south to join the larger Salt.

In places there were small farms adjoining the stream with post-rail fences to keep range stock out and irrigated by diverted water. The cornstalks stood in neat shocks dried brown like Indian tepees. I admired their neatness, but personally hoped Mr. Hainey stuck with stock raising. My summer of mowing hay had been enough farming for this cowboy for a long while.

Two riders with high-crown hats drew up their lathered horses when we met in the road. They looked Texas. Both wore leather cuff guards and pistols in new holsters. I doubted either one was as old as me. They were clean-shaven, and their hot horses looked fast.

"Howdy," the dark-haired one said, checking his hard-breathing sorrel and leaning on his saddle horn like he aimed to learn all about me.

"Evening," I said, wondering if I needed to start packing my Colt. These two had an air about them made the skin on my neck itch, and that never was a good sign.

"He ain't no pilgrim," the freckle-faced one said, almost disappointed-sounding.

"My name's H.B., I didn't catch yours." I waited for an answer.

The dark-haired one finally spoke. "Dobe's his name, mine's Jason."

"Guess you fellows work around here?" I asked, feeling on my guard still, for they hadn't softened their toughness. They weren't a bit friendly.

Dobe laughed out loud like a crazy person and then clamped his hand over his mouth. He drew a scowl of disapproval from his partner. I didn't like the fact they were trying to have me between them. This Dobe kept edging his horse around behind me.

"Sure we work. I never seen you before. What's your business in these parts?" Jason asked, leaning on his horn. His sorrel pawed his front hoof, anxious to be moving again. For a drover, he rode an expensive horse. The saddle was silver-mounted too.

"I've got a job," I said, growing wary of their sneaking ways as I tried to watch both of them.

"Doing what? Slopping hogs?" Dobe asked flippantly, then gave another funny laugh.

"I don't figure what I do is any of your damn business." I glared back at Jason just as hard as he stared at me. I figured he was the leader, and the stupid one would go on his lead. "Besides, your friend doesn't have any manners."

"You got a lot of nerve, H.B., whoever you are, making comments about my friend, and you unarmed." He motioned to my lack of packing an iron.

"I didn't stop you two in the road looking for trouble, and I'm not in a grand mood to be taking the brunt of either of your bad manners."

Dobe had maneuvered his horse close behind Short. I expected any minute for him to try something behind my back, but I also knew by the subtle shift under me, Short had him in mind. Dobe was in the poorest position a human could be. A true kicking horse understands his range, capability, and direction; Short was the king kicker of them all.

"What do you plan to do about it?" Jason's words were cut off when Short gave a large, deep grunt and went to kicking his hind heels and backing into horse and rider. A high-pitched whistle escaped Short's exposed yellow teeth. His attack grew furious. The thuds of his hooves on Dobe and his horse were solid.

In front of me, Jason's high-strung sorrel whirled in fright at old Short's sudden fury and nearly unseated his rider. Behind my back, Dobe was screaming, "He's broke my damn leg!"

I fumbled with the saddlebag strap and leaned back to come up with the black-handled Colt. Gun finally in my hand, the odds were more in my favor, and a wave of relief swept me.

"He's got a gun!" Jason shouted. Unseated, he clung desperately to his horse's neck for balance. Dobe hit the ground with a flop. His mount, wide-eyed and fearful of Short's fury, left in a dead run for Linter's Store. Dobe was lying on the road holding his leg and moaning. The fight was gone from the Texans.

I touched my hat with the gun barrel. "Good evening, gentlemen."

"Listen, you no-good . . ." Jason's threatening profanity followed me as I rode off. Short took my lead and we short-loped away from the pair. I took back all the bad things I ever said about my cranky cow pony and drove the Colt in my waistband. Next time I got back to Linter's I'd buy me a holster. Living on the North Cut would take some getting used to.

THE QUARTER CIRCLE Z was branded on the weathered board over the open gate. I let Short walk as we passed under it. I could clearly see the distant low ranch house and outbuildings under the mountain. Huddled up like they could survive the worst winter storm hurled down from the towering Mogollons, they had a homelike look that warmed me. I remembered the banty-legged little man I'd met in Phoenix and looked forward to seeing him again.

We forded the North Cut, the water hardly half-shin-deep on Short. Midstream, Short stopped to take some deep drafts of the river swirling around his legs, and then, with a vigorous shake that threatened to clap the stirrups against his belly, he waded out for the other side.

In the last light of day, I could hear the bark of a collie dog. I rode up and spotted Mr. Hainey standing in the center of the buildings and pens, with his weather-beaten Stetson in one hand and a switch in the other. He was nearly bent over and attempting to turn a black gilt back toward a corral.

"Mr. Hainey?" I asked.

"That's me," he said without looking up. "Get down and help me. I've spent an hour rounding her up, and she's plumb determined not to go in the pen."

"Certainly," I said, and stepped out of the saddle. Short snorted at the pig, but he remained ground-tied like he was trained to, though his opinion of the hog was obvious.

"Glad you're here, son. Dog!" the old man shouted to the overzealous collie who had made two or three false runs at the pig's rear. "Dog, you get back now!"

"H.B. Bentley, sir."

"I know, I hired you in Phoenix. Been expecting you. Dog! Damn you! Quit messing with her."

We were having a staring contest with Miss Pig. She would start left, Hainey'd wave his switch, then she'd start to go right, and he'd wave his hat. The tongue-lolling collie was on the ground to our right, but he could hardly contain himself. He wanted to bite the sow on the hams, which was exactly what we didn't want until we turned her snout toward the corral.

"She has a powerful mind," Mr. Hainey said.

"Hogs are like that," I agreed as we advanced a step at a time toward her. She still acted undecided. If she ever turned around, we'd spook her in the gate.

From the corner of my eye, I saw the collie bound up, and knew even Mr. Hainey's frantic shouting was too late. That dog could no longer stand the impasse, and in a growling blur of fury he leaped in and began to attack the black gilt's hind parts. Mr. Hainey shouted even louder for the dog to quit. The gilt issued ear-breaking screams under the dog's attack.

Pain blinds animals, and they quickly seek refuge from it. The only hole that pig could see was the hollow between Mr. Hainey's legs. The sow hit Mr. Hainey going fast and bowed him over her back. I saw Hainey's white handlebar mustache close to her tail. To my shock, he was holding on. Belly down, Mr. Hainey was riding that running sow away.

"Get a damn rope and catch her!" he hollered. "I'll ride her down."

I looked all around in the twilight and finally spotted a coil of rope on the corral. Over my shoulder, I could hear Hainey's cussing, the collie barking furiously after them. I whirled and rushed with the lariat in my hand across the open yard and around the shed, looking for the pig rider.

I found him looking disgusted as hell. He was sitting on his bottom at the base of a bushy juniper. The pig had run under the branches and stripped him off. I helped him up and handed him his hat.

"By Gawd, H.B., I believe that was the damn record." Hainey beat the dirt from his hat on his leg.

"What record?" I asked, hearing the collie still barking after the pig far down by the North Cut.

"That's the furthest I ever rode a damn pig."

I figured he was peeved at me for not coming quicker with the lariat. "I tried to get here."

"Hell, you done good. If I'd held on a little longer, we'd got that scutter back in the pen."

"Mr. Hainey, what now?" Did he want to track her down?

"Oh, we'll get her in the morning. That damn dog will be back after a while. I ought to kick his head in. He damn sure needs lots of training before roundup or we'll leave him home." He wrinkled his long, crooked nose at the pig smell that saturated his clothes. "Oh, just forget them for tonight. Let's go find some supper. You must be starved. She'll probably make us eat on the porch the way I stink."

"The missus?"

"No, she died years ago. Rosita's my housekeeper. She's more cantankerous than any wife."

"I see," I said, wanting to sound agreeable.

"You'll see, all right," he said, and clapped me on the shoulder as we walked back. "Nice to see you again, H.B. I was figuring you were due in any day."

"Let me tell you, it's good to be on a ranch again." Somewhere a whippoorwill was calling in the last

19

dusky light, and I smiled. Good to hear them again, too.

My Spanish was weak, but Hainey's housekeeper came out of the house babbling at fifty miles an hour, with some gusts to eighty. She was full-figured and wore a brown pleated shirt and a white peasant blouse that showed her thick cleavage. I imagined Rosita had been very beautiful as a girl. Even approaching forty, she had lots of charm. With her brown arms folded in front of her ample bust, she looked defiant enough for me.

"A bath? Woman, are you crazy?" Hainey asked. "Why, it's suppertime."

She gave him some more sharp Spanish words. I believed it was wash time at the Quarter Circle Z even if my boss wasn't convinced.

"This is H.B., the new hand," he said, like that would change her mind. He held out his big hat in my direction for her to look at me.

"I don't care who he is. He can take a bath too. I get you towels!" She stomped back in the house. Hainey slung his hat on his head. I wasn't going to say a word. A man takes a verbal whipping like that, he don't need anyone chiding him. I didn't know where, but we were going to bathe and change our clothes or we'd be fasting outside. Rosita had spoken.

Hainey had a couple sheepherder showers, tin tubs on the roof of one shed porch. They were filled by a temporary pipe from the windmill, and the water was sun-heated all day. Kind of handy—you pulled the chain for water on demand, and it wasn't ice-cold. The shower revived me.

After bathing and changing my clothes, I unsaddled Short and put him in the corral. Hainey carried my war bag, I hefted the saddle and bedroll. We stopped and he pushed open the door to the small quarters that were to be mine. Musty-smelling, but they'd do. I stowed my things inside. Last thing, I tossed the Colt on the bed. I damn sure didn't need it gouging my belly anymore, and Hainey's place seemed quiet enough. We went to the house to eat.

Rosita had little to say to us. She fussed over all the food she'd put out on the candlelit large table. Hainey indicated a seat for me, and he sat at the head chair. I stowed my hat and he asked grace. I saw Rosita cross herself when he finished.

"How was your trip up here?" he asked, finishing with the bowl of corn and passing it to me.

"Uneventful until today," I explained. I filled my plate as Rosita hovered over us like a mother hen, handing this and that if she thought we even were thinking about it. The beans I ladled out were rich and spicy, the boiled corn sweet, and the thick bacon on the platter was crisp. Between fixing and bites, I tried to casually explain my meeting with Ewell Rice.

"He ordered you out of the country, huh?" I saw the amusement in Hainey's twinkling eyes as he fed himself.

"Then I met Stout, and she asked me to the Pecan School House dance. Is it far from here?"

"No, it ain't far, but she must think you're all right

if she did that. Those Rice girls ain't got much use for most of the young men in this country."

"Do you reckon if we get caught up . . . ?"

"Sure, you can go this Saturday night. You'll need to get out and meet some young people."

"Thanks," I said, enjoying my new boss more by the minute.

"Is he going to dig the new hole for the outhouse?" Rosita asked.

"Dammit, Rosy, can't you let the poor boy eat in peace? You'll ruin his appetite with your list of things that need done around here."

"You told me!" She looked about to become mad.

I smiled to myself. The food was delicious, the company friendly, and she wasn't going to put a wet blanket on my having a fine time, though the outhouse project sounded like the unspoken part of this job.

"Know anything about two smart-talking Texans, Jason and Dobe?" I asked, grasping the thick coffee mug in both hands and enjoying the warmth.

Hainey looked up, with a hardness in his deep-set eyes. "Where did you meet them?"

"On the road south of here. Why?"

"They work for a rancher over east. Kinda tough-acting?"

I agreed. "Is it about this rustling business Rice spoke about?"

"It's more than rustling now. Two men have been killed in the last three months. I think they knew too much. Someone is slipping cattle out of this country, rebranding them, and selling them either to the Indian

Agencies or at the railhead in Flag." Hainey shook his head, and then he replaced the thin gray hair that fell down in his face. "Mighty serious. What happened between you and the Texas boys?"

"They wanted to pick a fight with me from the moment I stopped to meet them. The dumber one, Dobe, tried to sneak around behind me and try something. When he managed to do that, my horse, Short, kicked him and his horse. Dobe has a very sore leg, and Jason's horse nearly threw him off. I drew my Colt and bid them good-bye."

Hainey smiled at me. "You had a sight of things happen in your first day. Who's that hollering outside?"

I heard someone hailing the house. The collie was back and barking too. I saw Rosita exchange a questioning frown with Hainey.

"You be careful, Zack," she said with a concerned look as Hainey stood up and started for the front door. I rose to follow him, wishing to hell I had my handgun. The soberness on both of their faces told me they were on edge about any arrival.

Hainey picked up a Winchester from beside the door and levered a shell in the chamber before he went out. I followed, feeling very vulnerable passing through the halo of light while stepping out on the dark porch.

"It's me, Zack! Charlie Brackett!"

"Damn, Charlie. Make a man get up from his supper. Come on in. He's a neighbor," he said for my sake, and handed me the long gun. "It's all right."

23

I took the rifle back inside and nodded at Rosita. She looked recovered, but why were they so edgy about someone riding up? There had to be a good reason. Zack Hainey didn't seem the type to fear much of anything.

Hainey introduced me to the rancher, a man in his forties, near six foot tall, narrow-waisted with a black shadow of a beard. He wore a gun on his hip. Brackett took a seat, and Rosita went for more coffee.

"Zack, they slow-elked a big roan heifer of yours. I found her this morning near the Blue Springs Tank." The man looked hard at Hainey as if waiting for a reply.

I could see a lot of anger in my new boss's face. "Damn, they can't take steers, they have to take good she-stock." He set down his fork and looked deep in thought.

"Yeah, it's kinda like they want to make us mad."

"You know who's killing them?" I asked, looking first at Hainey, then at Brackett, for an answer. I knew the slow-elking business Brackett spoke of meant the butchers only took the hindquarters, a wasteful practice even for rustlers.

Brackett looked at Zack, then back at me. "I say it's them damn Mormon dirt farmers."

"We can't prove that, Charlie," Hainey said. "It could be someone wants us to have a war with them folks. Whoever's doing it damn sure has tried to spark it. And besides, you ain't got one shred of evidence them Mormons are even involved."

Brackett busied himself eating as if he was sullied

up and wouldn't speak anymore on the subject. I stopped for a moment to consider all I knew about the deal. Ewell Rice thought I'd been part of the element getting his stock. This whole country was full of folks suspicious of one another. The pair on the road came to mind, but they weren't smart enough to do all this.

"I'll ride up there at first light and identify her so I can take her out of my logbook," Hainey said. "No clear tracks, huh?"

"No, but by God, Zack, one day I'll catch one of them doing it, and you'll come help me hang them, won't you?" Brackett demanded.

"Yes, I will," Mr. Hainey said softly.

On my bunk an hour later, I studied the moon-lighted, cobwebbed glass panes. A silver light shone in the bunkhouse window and illuminated the floor. I speculated on what the other two Rice girls looked like. Was one of them prettier than Stout? And I thought about Brackett's hard question and Mr. Hainey's answer, a quiet and cold "yes." I only saw one man hung, and I saw him over and over in my sleep. I laid my face down on the goose-down pillow and prayed I didn't dream of that lynching again, especially in my first night on the Quarter Circle Z.

❖ 3 ❖

The new hole for the outhouse was barely six inches deep. I'd pickaxed for hours at the unyielding ground till my back and arms ached. I paused to use my kerchief to wipe the sweat off my face. Mr. Hainey had ridden out earlier that morning to check on the wasted heifer. As I studied the wood-frame structure beside me, I really looked forward to having the unpainted two-holer drug over astraddle the new pit and this job finished. I went back to swinging the backbreaking pick, with little to show for each effort.

The collie heralded Hainey's return, and I barely looked up to see him arrive on a head-nodding dun. Filled with regret over my inability to impress him with my labors, I drew a deep breath and straightened up to await his opinion.

"How are you coming?" he asked, leaning over in the saddle to study the hole.

"Terrible, this ground is harder than a rock."

"I've got the cure for that. I'll be right back." He rode off and in a few minutes returned packing a red wooden box marked BLASTING STICKS and carrying the familiar name of the Adams Powder Company. I was about to hug him. He had the solution to my problem.

"You got a lot of that?" I asked, realizing that his way would be much easier than mine.

"This box full, that should do it." He nodded and set the box down. "Got to handle this stuff easy, though, or it'll scatter us over half a section. A heavy blow or shock and it'll go off."

I agreed and stepped out of the shallow hole. He was opening the top of the box and drew out a red waxy stick. Expertly he pried on the end, boring a hole down in the tube with his jackknife, and stuffed in some cord for a fuse.

"We need a hole made to stuff this in," he said. "There's a star drill in the toolshed."

I left at a jog to find it. The notion of using blasting sticks had my sore muscles feeling better every step of the way. I located the eighteen-inch bit and hurried back. We hammer-drilled a hole for the explosive. That completed, Hainey painstakingly placed the waxy stick in and packed around it. He was very careful not to bother the fuse that ran out of the end. On his britches leg, Hainey struck a lucifer match and then touched the flame to the cord. It was lighted and smoldering. We ran around to the front of the bunkhouse, holding our ears with our palms to protect them from the blast.

"Always takes longer than you think for those fuses to burn up," he said to reassure me when it didn't instantly go off. Both of us were set and looking away, anticipating the blast.

"Any minute." I clinched my jaw so it was tight and I kinda hunched forward, waiting.

The explosion was more of a soft puff. Hainey frowned at me. Had it gone off? Neither of us were sure, so we carefully went back to the corner of the bunkhouse and peeked at the damage. The explosion had barely loosened the dirt around the drilled hole. Oh, damn! I just knew I'd spend the rest of the fall and part of the winter picking the hole deep enough to use.

"This calls for severe measures," Mr. Hainey announced. "We ain't spending all year digging no damn crapper hole."

I agreed. He was a man of my own sentiments. We jumped in and began to drill holes for twelve sticks of dynamite. The drilling went slow. Rosita came by. After a few curt words with her brown lip curled, she left us alone and began hanging her wash on the line nearby.

"You found the heifer?" I asked him.

"Yes, she'd been butchered several days ago. Varmints had eat on her a lot," Hainey said, fixing the other sticks with fuses. "I also saw that black sow down by the North Cut. We'll have to get her up later on."

"There were no clues around where they killed the heifer?"

"No, the tracks were too old."

It seemed like two hours before we had the holes made and the blasting sticks put in them. His setup looked very effective to me. Hainey set the rest of the box of explosives on the dirt pile nearby, and we went to work. Twelve fuses were tied together, all of them leading to the main one.

"Get out of the hole. This is going to shake that dirt," he assured me. Hainey struck the match. I smiled as he lighted the main fuse. A small sparking flame consumed the paper twisted string containing black gunpowder. We were going to have a real Chinese New Year out of this one. He caught up with me around the corner of the bunkhouse. We covered our ears and waited. Mr. Hainey had a big grin of anticipation, with both his palms compressed over his ears. Success was only a few seconds away. We exchanged another confident nod. We had it made.

The first explosion was earthshaking. A cloud of dust rose in the sky over the bunkhouse. The second one was equally spectacular. But soon pieces of boards and wood shingles came raining down. So much fell, we were forced to run to the bunkhouse porch for our own protection. In the rain of stones, dirt, wood bits and pieces, I looked at Mr. Hainey, and he looked at me. The storm over, we rushed around the corner to survey the damage. Through the dust and smoke I could see the front door and part of the outhouse's roof was blown away. Worse, Rosita's wash looked the brown-red color of the dirt.

"Damn!" Hainey swore. "We left that box of blasting sticks too close."

The hole dug out easy. Then Mr. Hainey and I spent the rest of the day repairing the outhouse after we moved it to its new spot.

"Always remember, that damn blasting powder is dangerous," he reminded me as we carried the carpenter tools back to the shed.

"What about Rosita and her wash?" I asked, wondering if she'd even feed us after her angry tirade about what we did to her wash.

"Her bark's worse than her bite," Hainey said with a sly smile, and we went to the house for supper.

Hainey talked some more about the troubles in the country during supper. Mormon farmers had homesteaded the farmable land. Cattlemen had made homesteads, too, for their headquarters and ran their cattle outside on the free range. He explained a lot of tension had grown between the two forces, and Hainey disliked the fact they were nearly at war.

"Plumb different than when I came here. Why, fifteen years ago, me and the Apaches had this country to ourselves," Hainey said.

"They ever bothered you?" I asked, curious about those times.

"I fed them beef for my being here."

"Did they take a lot?"

"No, and they never killed one and wasted it either."

"He was too good to them!" Rosita said in clear English.

"Now, Rosita, that ain't so. I gave them a fair price for you."

I must have blinked my eyes, and Hainey nodded yes to my surprise.

"Tell him," he said to her.

"You tell him yourself. You did it," she said, and left the room as if in a huff.

"What happened?"

"They came by one morning. A half dozen bucks. They had unblocked hats and greasy eagle feathers in the bands, their rifles all studded up with copper tacks. Jewelry made out of Mexican silver coins hung around their neck. There was this chief called Mule with them. He spoke some English, and I first figured they wanted a little tobacco or some pork. I'd given them a half side of bacon before. There wasn't much game left in the country for them to hunt.

"Mule, he says, 'you want a squaw?' I really didn't want one. My wife had died two years before that. And I was used to living in a house, and most Apache women weren't. So I told him no."

"He had Rosita for a prisoner then?" I asked in disbelief.

"I didn't know it was her. You kinda got to guess sometimes what a dang Apache means when he talks."

"Well, how did you get her?" I could hardly hold still for the answer.

"He brought her here the next day and said he wanted three good horses for her."

"You traded with him."

"I only gave him two. She was acting mad as a wet

31

hen, and I figured with all her barking, he probably
wanted to be rid of her worse than he'd admit to me."
Hainey laughed aloud, and Rosita came back in the
room shaking her head at him.

"He didn't tell you all of it," she said, and turned
her head from looking at him. "He quickly took me
home to my people in Mexico, but my husband and
my children were dead. Killed in a raid. I felt so bad
and all alone, so I let him bring me back to this crazy
place with him."

"She ain't regretted a minute of it, have you?"
Hainey asked, breaking into laughter.

I saw her genuinely smile at him as she started to
pick up the dishes. "I wasn't very smart coming back
here," she said, and left us alone.

"Tomorrow, H.B., we'll round up the horses we'll
need for roundup and shoe them," Hainey announced.

"I hope you don't blow them up and cover my wash
with dirt again," Rosita said from the kitchen doorway.

"Don't lose no sleep over that, sister. Not a chance
in this world," Hainey said, rolling himself a cigarette
and passing the makings to me. We went out on the
porch to smoke and listened to the cicadas hissing. It
was a nice way to end the day.

"There's lots of folks for you to meet in this valley,"
Hainey offered. "Kenyons are pure Texas, that's who
Dobe and Jason work for. They're on the east range.
Dewain Kenyon is a little mouthy for his own good,
but aside from hiring worthless trash, I don't know

much more bad about them. He has the Two X K brand that takes the side of a steer to put it on."

"Brackett and Rice share this side of the range with you?" I asked, orienting myself with the lay of the outfits.

"Yeah, they do. We better turn in. Can you shoe horses?" he asked.

"Sure," I quickly answered. I liked shoeing horses, and we had some to do the next day. It would beat picking out a new outhouse hole all to hell.

The collie followed me to the bunkhouse and plopped down on the porch. Reckon he and I'd made friends that day. Hainey never petted him, and I hoped he didn't get mad because I had to pet the friendly dog. I went to bed remembering some good dogs I'd owned. But sleep quickly consumed me.

I awoke to the triangle's ring before dawn. The collie was on the porch wagging his tail. I named him Bobby. I washed my face and hands on the back porch of the main house and was grateful for the flannel shirt—there was a touch of fall in the mountain air.

Rosita had eggs, side meat fried brown, and lots of sourdough biscuits to lather with her cow butter as well as plenty of strong coffee. Hainey got him a bargain, two horses for such a good cook. I wondered what Injuns ate, but I decided in the reality at hand, this meal was to last me till dark if we were out rounding up horses.

After we finished eating, we rose, and I decided to

ask the man. "Mr. Hainey, do I need to wear that Colt of mine, sir?"

He studied me for a long moment. "I ain't paying you gunfighter's wages."

"Mr. Hainey, I ride for the brand. My daddy said you either ride for the brand or check out. Any threat to you or your place and livestock is a threat to me."

"I can handle things myself." Hainey stopped and considered my offer. "H.B., your old daddy must've had lots of savvy in this world. I figured you was a good man that was lost when I seen you in Phoenix unloading that hay. But promise me one thing?"

"Yes, sir?"

"Don't jump into nothing we can walk away from, you savvy that?"

"I do, sir."

"Good, let's ride. Them old horses ain't seen me in four months. Some ain't been rode since last fall." He slammed on his hat, buckled on his sidearm, and I hurried to the bunkhouse for mine. When I stuck the Colt down in my waistband I had a strange feeling. Hard to describe, but it was like a dark cloud went over my head and left me a little weaker or bothered. I wasn't sure which one.

We found his horses with some other stock in a grassy basin about midmorning. He pointed out a tall blood bay.

"We need to catch him. He usually gets away, and he's a powerful horse to drag in those bigger three-year-old steers that get wild."

I studied the country and figured the horses would

probably swing to the north. I wasn't certain where they'd go from there if we fell in after them.

"What you thinking, H.B.?"

"Well, sir, they're your horses, but I figure you set in after them, they'll circle back, and I can capture that bay with Short here."

Hainey nodded and the plan was set. I figured that old man knew more in his little finger about horses than I would ever know, but he was testing me. I aimed to prove I could do it.

He rode off to bring them around and give me a chance to gather the bay when the band circled back east along the base of the hill. I uncoiled the best rope I'd taken from the corral that morning early, one of several I had brought to capture horses with.

Short knew something was happening. He kept laying down his ears and stomping with his hind foot to show he was ready. Since his bucking fit he threw at the Daniels' (except for kicking Dobe), he'd been acting almost too good. I formed a big loop in the lariat and studied the dust coming. Hainey was driving them back against the base of the hill. I set spurs in Short, and he bounded forward like a big jackrabbit. Loop in my right hand held wide and ready, I urged Short on. He had lots of speed, and at a sprint there wasn't much that could outdistance him.

The bay saw us coming and tried to change directions. Short seemed to know that was his goal. I whirled the lariat over my head as Short closed the distance. The bay realized his situation and desperately tried to scramble up the eroded bank. I threw the loop and it nested around his head, but to my dismay, Short never stopped. I jerked on the reins with my left hand, to no avail. Short cat-hopped up the bank past the bay horse. The bay was spooked and turned away from us. I was busy dallying around the horn to shorten the rope. I figured he'd jerk Short over backward if he ever lunged away and had enough slack. Where was that stupid horse of mine going? Then the rope went taut over my leg, and the action drew Short to his knees instead of over backwards as I had dreaded. Stopped at last, I breathed easier, weak with the knowledge my stubborn horse nearly had us both killed.

The bay was on his back on the hillside and flaying the air with his hooves. Short found his footing and turned to face the bay as he struggled up. The bay finally lunged up to his feet and shook the dirt and dust from his hide. The tumble was educational for him; I could see a whole lot of sense in his eyes compared to the wild-eyed horse I'd roped only seconds before. Past education comes back fast to a horse.

"He won't try that again," Hainey said, leaning on his saddle horn and admiring my capture.

I didn't want him to dwell on it. I called it luck to myself. Actually, I had figured Short and me were going to be thrown for a bad spill because of his cussedness. Just so the boss was impressed.

"The others?" I asked.

"We'll trail them home. They know where to go and will do it without him to lead them astray. That bay will come, too, won't he?" Hainey smiled and gave me a nod of approval.

"Yes, sir," I said. I fashioned a halter for the hard-blowing big horse. He still had lots of devil in him, and I thought for a moment Short was going to fight with him. There was a quick show of teeth and ears-back fury, but the two geldings fell in—suspicious of each other—and we trailed in the thin dust raised by the rest of the horses.

Late afternoon, we had them bunched and trotting. I could see they were good using horses, but I expected a rancher like Hainey to keep good ones. He went to swinging his lariat, and we sent them loping the last mile home. Making a lot of dust, we were rocking along in the saddle, bringing the herd in. A good day.

We rounded the last corral, and I thought we were home free. That moment the black gilt rushed out of nowhere and across the yard right in front of the horses, with barking Bobby in hot pursuit. They always told me a horse had a one-track mind, and don't never disturb it too sudden like. That pig and angry dog were too much. The horse herd split and put on a new burst of speed to avoid the barking, screaming ball in their path.

I dallied up the bay closer, while two sorrels and a gray broke to the left at the bunkhouse.

"Sweet Jesus!" Hainey shouted, but even his burst of speed to head them off was too late. He rounded the bunkhouse whipping and riding in hot pursuit but way behind them. His dun was nearly on his side, pawing and digging as hard as he could go.

When the loose horses hit it, I first heard the snap. Then I saw the clothesline go high enough up so you could see it over the bunkhouse roof. Then it fell like a wet noodle decorated with sheets and clothing. That meant Rosita's rewash was on the ground. We were into it again.

❖ 4 ❖

Rosita used a flatiron on my best white shirt. She volunteered to do it on Friday, and when she brought it out, that shirt sparkled white and was stiff enough to stand in the corner. Like it was planned, Mr. Hainey and I wound up the horseshoeing midday Saturday.

"I guess you're taking up Stout's invite, huh?" Hainey asked as we washed our hands.

"Unless you got more to do?" I glanced over at him. Hainey was drying his hands on the coarse towel Rosita had hung out for us.

"No, you go along. Why, if I was twenty-two or so, you'd have to tie me up in the shed to keep me around here on Saturday evening."

"Reckon I'll be twenty-four come December."

"Not a bad guess. Let's eat so you can ride on up there and not miss anything."

"You got any advice?"

Hainey stopped in the door and looked back. "Watch that pair, Jason and Dobe, they kinda itch for trouble. They're bullies, so I'd say take your gun along. Shame a man can't just go enjoy himself." Hainey shook his head regretfully. "Of course, them Mormon boys sometimes get pretty possessive of their sisters."

"I know, don't shoot my way out of anything I can walk away from."

Hainey nodded like the words pleased him and went inside. I was itching to get on, but I ate lunch with them and then excused myself for a quick bath.

Dressed up, I saddled the big bay. Hainey thought he needed a lot of riding out, and the trip would gentle him some. Wearing my starched shirt and my brown suit coat all brushed, my hat wiped clean with a damp rag, I waved at the two of them and set out for the Pecan School House. The bay humped a little at first, but he settled into a long swinging walk, and my thoughts were on the Rice girls and the evening ahead.

Pecan School House stood in a grove of stately pecans nearly bare of leaves with clusters of nuts in splitting hulls on the branches. Whitewashed, the frame building shone in the golden sun, with children running about playing games. There were several wagons around the broad yard's perimeter. I didn't see the Rices', so I started riding around the grounds to find them, tipping my hat at ladies and exchanging hi's with family members. Many had brought bedding, so

I assumed they would stay the night. There were cooking fires with wives tending pots hung over them, and most everyone was cordial to my howdy. Several pretty doe-eyed teen girls turned away when I greeted them and touched my hat, being respectful. No shortage of attractive women, I noticed. Several nearly grown boys either smiled or ignored me.

"Look who's here," Stout said, standing with her hands on her hips. She wore a blue checkered dress—a much softer look without her duster, pants, and hat. Her brown hair looked hard-brushed, and red highlights glistened in the light filtering through the spiderlike limbs of the overhead pecan tree.

"Am I late?" I asked, dismounting.

"No, actually you're early, but that's fine," Stout said. "Here, I want you to meet the rest of the family. This is Tate."

Tate was the youngest. Her wide brown eyes beneath demure thick lashes made her the pretty teen. She even blushed under her older sister's insistence she shake hands with me. In her thick, curly hair she wore ribbons, and her figure had a girlish look in the deep brown dress that complemented her. She was pretty and she was young.

"Nice to meet you," I said with my hat in my left hand.

"Yes," she said, unsure of what else to say.

"Meet Erv," Stout said.

I looked into the prettiest gray-blue eyes I'd ever seen. Erv's face was oval and much softer than her older sister's. Her high cheeks were nearly raw from being out in the elements. Her light brown hair was bobbed like a Dutch boy's. The style flattered her. I even noticed her long, slender nose had been broken and had a slight curve in it. She stood half a head shorter than me, and her willowy figure was clothed in a powder blue dress.

"How's Mr. Hainey?" she asked, shaking my hand.

"Doing fine. My first week at his place has sure been exciting."

"It has?" she asked.

"Oh, yes," I said, grateful she would talk to me. "First off, Mr. Hainey rode a hog all over."

Their laughter only encouraged me, and I went from feeling like the outsider to being part of their group. But I couldn't hardly keep from staring at Erv. Not many women ever had that effect on me. My guts even rolled around thinking about her. The three girls' smiling faces and laughter warmed me in the long rays of late afternoon. We shared some yarns, and soon I was lulled into relaxing some more, like I belonged with them.

"Unsaddle your old bay," Stout finally said. "We'll have some food ready in a few minutes. Paw's coming too."

I saw Ewell Rice coming across the clearing on a bald-face horse. He was stopping to visit and reached down to shake hands with friends. I wondered if he'd be half as happy as Stout and the girls to see me. Nothing I could do about that, though I dreaded the notion of meeting him again after our last tangle.

I set my saddle on its end and hobbled the bay. Ewell joined me and began unsaddling his cow pony.

"I guess you're Bentley?" he asked, pausing with his arms full of saddle and pads.

My hand shot out, and he switched the saddle to grip mine. "I guess we got off to a bad start?"

"No, Mr. Rice, I could have acted better. I understand your worries now; Mr. Hainey told me all about the troubles up here," I said.

"I didn't know you were Zack's man then either. He filled you in on our troubles?"

"Yes, he also lost a heifer to elkers last week."

Rice made a distasteful face and shook his head. He set the saddle down and cleared his throat with a deep growl. "This roundup may show how many we really are missing. May even break some of us if the cattle we expect ain't out there."

"Someone will catch them," I said, anxious to go back to the company of the girls but not wanting to show that part.

"Both of them are dead. Chuck Mains and Thad Buckner are in the cemetery. They probably both discovered too much."

"Hainey told me two men were killed over this."

Rice squinted his eyes, and I turned to view the two cowboys whipping their horses in a neck-and-neck race to the front of the schoolhouse. Without regard for the playing children or anyone else, they lashed their mounts to the last minute, then reined their cow ponies to a sliding halt against the building. It was Jason and Dobe.

"Ain't they dandies?" Rice asked with a distasteful scowl on his bearded face. "They keep on, they'll get lined out."

"Come eat," Tate said.

We followed her. I waited for Rice to wash at the pan set out on the tailgate for us. Erv handed me a towel, and I looked a little too long into her pale blue eyes. She turned without an expression. It was my turn to wash.

Stout fixed her father a dish from the large kettle over the fire, then she handed me a tin plate of steaming brown beans. They smelled mouth-watering good and I thanked her.

I jerked around at these words. "H.B., huh? You wearing your damn gun?"

The hot plate was hurting my hands as I looked up at Jason on his horse. I wanted to hurl the scalding beans up in Jason's taunting face. He had his hand on his gun butt as he sat his sorrel.

"Get out of here, you Texas trash!" Ewell Rice demanded. He waded in between us, and Jason's sorrel even backed at his fury. "If you ain't got any better manners than that, I'll jerk you off the horse and beat some into you."

Jason retreated, and I quickly set the plate down on the tailgate. Grateful to escape the heat, I hated for Rice having to interfere. Briskly I rubbed my palms on my jeans—they hurt. I watched Jason turn in the saddle to glance back at me, all the hatred still in his eyes.

"You all right?" Stout asked, rushing over. She took

my hand and examined it like a mother hen. "Sorry, I didn't mean to burn you. Why didn't you drop it?"

"And waste good beans? I'm fine," I said to reassure her, but I drew a peevish look from her when she released my wrist.

"That Texas trash. See why I was so damn mad at Linter's?" Rice said. "I figured you were another one of them. You get crossed with him too?"

"Both of them," I said, blowing on my beans and remembering what I'd promised Hainey; there'd be no shooting when I could walk away from it. Jason might make that hard. But I'd left my Colt in the saddlebags for the moment.

The sun was setting and a cool evening breeze swept up the long valley. Fiddle music wafted out from the schoolhouse. The "Red River Valley" tune brought a lot of nice memories back. I waited while the girls made last-minute adjustments to each other's dresses. Their paw had gone off to see some rancher buddies. Being my first dance up there, I wondered if Erv had a fellow waiting for her in the hall. I hoped not.

Tate seemed to bubble, and Stout acted like the boss hen I expected. Erv looked the most reserved. I was trying to not look at her, for she quickly looked away when I did catch her eye. Courtship at times gets dumb and downright awkward. I felt like I was a wooden block as the four of us headed for the beckoning doorway. Other women wearing bonnets and shawls were coming with their menfolk. I noticed the Rice girls were bareheaded and guessed all they had were their cowboy hats to wear. It didn't bother me.

The benches were lined along the walls, and Stout indicated where she wanted me to lead them halfway down the side of the room. There was a cast-iron stove near the teacher's stage where the musicians were seated. A wagon wheel chandelier of lit candles furnished the light. Long shadows flitted among the cobwebbed rafters.

I sat beside Stout, Erv and Tate to the right, all with our hands in our laps like we weren't sure what to do with ourselves. I was grateful when the fiddler began to play the "Westphalia Waltz." Stout turned to face me. We both spoke at the same time. Our actions drew soft laughter from all of us.

"Want to dance?" I asked. Stout nodded, nearly hitting my hat brim with her head, she was so close.

I'd done lots of dancing, some around schoolhouse gatherings like this, some when I was full of whiskey and hugging a buxom saloon gal. I never amounted to no expert, but I could waltz. My right hand on the valley in Stout's back, we waltzed around the room. I forgot Erv, I forgot Jason and his idiot friend, and we swung around the schoolhouse. I was shocked at her skill. Stout certainly was light and graceful on her feet.

After the number, we returned to our spot on the bench, and Stout drew Erv to her feet and put her hand in mine. The music hadn't even begun—the musicians were arguing over what to play next.

I could see Erv was uncomfortable, but I didn't know why, and didn't know why none of the boys came by and asked the Rice girls to dance. Several long drinks of water hung out near the doorway with their backs to the wall, and I figured a few more trips outside to their secreted bottle and they'd get their nerve up and wander over.

The music started and I lifted Erv's left arm to begin dancing. She looked into my eyes, and I guess I could have stood there for the whole dance doing that, but we made two stumbling steps instead, then let go and laughed at our own awkwardness. I don't know if anyone saw us; they might have. She quickly recovered and we were off. I once saw a picture in a bar of a cowboy dancing with an angel. Erv was that heavenly a partner, and if there were twenty couples on the floor or two, I never noticed as we whirled around.

"I'm clumsy," she said.

I blinked in disbelief. "That's not so."

"You're very kind, H.B."

"How come no one asks you girls to dance?" I blurted it out, and regretted it as soon as I did.

"We're those Rice girls," she said with distaste.

"Oh," I said, wishing I'd never asked her that. Across the room I saw Jason standing before Tate. He looked like a banty rooster, and I saw a gleam in Tate's eyes over the attention the Texan showed in her.

"What's wrong?" Erv asked.

"Jason's asking Tate to dance."

"Oh," she said, and looked away from my glance at her as we waltzed around to the tune. "Don't worry, Stout can handle him."

She was right. I settled back at my respectable distance of her in my arms and swung her around to the fiddle's refrains. I thought she let go of a little of her rigidity as we danced, but she stiffened again when the dance was over and we headed back.

Jason was not around. The two seated Rice girls smiled at us and began to include Erv in their talk about who all was there. I drew Tate for the next dance, and I had a flare-up of remembering dancing with my little sister again.

"Jason want to dance?" I asked, noticing she was looking for someone.

"I guess," she said. We both spotted him and a partner. It was the attractive doe-eyed girl I'd seen earlier around the wagons.

"That's Darling Moore. She's a Mormon," Tate said quickly. The rest of the time she tried to avoid looking at him. I almost smiled at her reaction. I didn't know what Stout had done to run the Texan off, but with my dislike for Jason, I'd have sure helped her. Obvious that wasn't Tate's wishes, though, but she was young.

At the first break we sipped lemonade—sweet syrupy lemonade with a whang that cleared your throat and solved your thirst. This time Stout and Erv helped the women serve, with folks drinking and returning the cups for others to use.

I was thoroughly enjoying myself, having three skilled women to dance with me. Only after we were seated and waiting did I notice that the girls all wore their pointy-toed riding boots that peeked out from under the hem of their dresses. Of course, it didn't bother me, but they tried to hide the fact like they were too poor to own ladylike shoes. Women worry about the dangedest things, even tomboys turned ladies.

The dance was over way too soon. We exited orderly out the door, me kinda herding the tribe.

"H.B., you get the hell away from those women's skirts!" Jason ordered.

The crowd sort of drew their breath. He stood in the starlight with his hands on his hip about thirty yards from the front porch. Everyone drew back.

"I'm unarmed," I said, shaking my head at Stout that I could handle this.

"Get a gun!" Jason ordered.

"Why don't you just hang yours up and we'll solve this with our fists."

"Boys, boys!" someone protested, but he quickly backed away when Jason turned with his threatening hand on his gun butt.

"Well?" I asked, removing my coat and hat, and handing them to Erv. This rift between us needed to be settled. I wasn't going to get in any gunplay with him. Besides, Jason wasn't drunk enough and didn't seem to be that big a fool to shoot me down before this many people. That would be suicide. They'd string him up.

"I'll whip you to death," he said, unbuckling his gun belt. I felt better when he passed it off to someone and stripped off his coat and threw his hat down. We were equal then, and I advanced on him.

"I'm going to teach you a lesson," Jason bragged.

He stepped in. I blocked his shot and drove my fist in his gut. He drew back, but his wind was short. I knew I'd hurt him. He danced barely out of my reach while he recovered. Two blows like that and he'd doubled over.

Jason came in again in a fury of fists. One fist hit my cheek, and I pounded his ear hard enough to stagger him sideways. But I tasted salty blood from a blow he'd landed on my mouth. I followed him to close the fight. My fists were battering him hard, and he was retreating.

Then someone was on my back. Dobe cursing me as he grappled to get hold of me. He tried to pin my arms and finally managed to get his arms around my waist. I smashed his foot with a bootheel, fighting off Jason, who had come back hard after his friend's interception.

The crowd was complaining. Dobe had me in a bear hug and was dragging me down from behind. Jason was hammering my face.

"Get off him, you no-good rat!" Stout said sharply over my shoulder. Without time to look, I felt her pull Dobe off, and without him for an anchor, I waded into Jason with newfound fury. But he darted back and away. Like so many fights, this one could go on for hours and not prove a thing.

Folks were laughing. I dared look for a moment. Stout had Dobe by a handful of hair and was kicking the hell out of his sore leg. You could hear Dobe's screaming. I took a solid lick on my cheek from my opponent for the pleasure of seeing Dobe's plight. But

I didn't let that slow me, and attacked Jason until he backed away. When I checked again, Dobe was on his knees minding her.

"You through fighting?" I asked Jason.

"Yeah," he said, holding his jaw where I'd managed a hard punch. "Next time you better be wearing a damn gun, Bentley."

"Next time I'll use a wagon slat on you."

Stout gave Dobe a swift kick in the butt and sent him stumbling off. I thanked Stout, and thanked Erv for holding my coat and hat. She nodded, and we walked in silence back to their wagon.

"Dobe's sore leg will be hurting him again after Stout got through with him. I appreciate your help." The girls laughed aloud as we headed across the yard.

"That bully'll think next time before he jumps in like that again," Stout said.

"Sorry you had my troubles," I said.

Tate swung on her oldest sister's arm and said, "Gosh no, H.B. At least we got to dance tonight. Usually only some old men asks us, maybe once all night, and Lord knows we been practicing all the time for a night like this to happen."

"Tate!" Erv said to hush her sister.

"Thanks anyway for the meal and letting me step on your toes," I said, amused at Tate's honesty. I could see those girls practicing with each other.

"You going home tonight?" Stout asked.

"I planned to," I said.

"They'll have a bonfire and tell stories most of the

night. Next time bring your bedroll, stay all night, and we'll fix you breakfast the next morning."

"You've got a deal. Guess I'll see you Monday morning at camp?"

"We'll be there," Stout said. "You ride home careful like."

I tossed my saddle on the bay and cinched him up. I hated to leave their company. It had been a long while since I'd had that much fun. I touched my face— I'd have a bruise where Jason had slugged me. When I swung my leg over the bay, I regretted the night wasn't longer. Each Rice sister shook my hand. Erv even gave me a very quick smile when I reached down and took her hand. That picture was enough to ride home with me in the starlight.

❧ 5 ❧

Charlie Brackett and a toothless wrangler by the
name of Sonny Pitts brought their horses to the
Hainey place on Sunday afternoon. I had spent most
of the day saddling our stock and being certain they
were saddle-wise enough to use. A blaze-faced sorrel
and the gray broke into a few jumps, but nothing like
Short could do. I had all but one of the lot of them
settled down and acting good in half an hour. A
horse's learning comes back fast with firm hands and
good equipment.

"Folks tell me you're quite a dancer," Charlie said,
leaning his chin on the corral rail.

I glanced at him as I cinched up the girth on the
last range horse left to dust off: a dish-faced dun that
acted half-walleyed.

"I didn't see you there," I said, dropping the stirrup,
preparing to mount the dun.

"I talked to some folks coming home from there. Lots of them were sore about that Texan calling you out. Said he was just looking for trouble."

I nodded and swung up. In the end, Jason and his sidekick would have to be settled with someday. I certainly hoped they went off for good and left me alone. My thinking distracted by my concerns, I woke up in a storm as the lineback horse threw a tantrum. The dun bogged his head in the sand, and we made two rounds around the corral, with me pulling hard on the reins and him firmly but surely crow-hopping for all he was worth.

"Open the gate!" I shouted, and they did. I let the horse have his head, and we were racing full tilt across the open grass country south of the ranch. He finally gave up racing and flat loped. Then I whipped and spurred him hard to go again. I wanted all that silliness out of his hide before we left the ranch. He'd get tired being the wild fool in a hurry.

I had lots of time to think on things like how I'd have to handle Jason and his pard the next time we met. They'd need a better lesson than the halfhearted fistfight of the previous night, maybe like paw said about an egg-sucking pup we had. Some never learned to stop it, and you had to kill them. The notion didn't appeal to me, but I was tired of Jason and Dobe's mouthing. Maybe they'd drift out of the country; their kind did things like that. I gave the sweaty dun a nudge with my rowels, and we short-loped back to the pens.

I swung my saddle off and turned the dun in with

the others. Hainey and Charlie came down from the house. I knew they wanted to talk from the looks on their faces.

"You know, H.B., you done real good at that dance not letting that Jason egg you into a gunfight. But he'll be back."

"I know that fight didn't resolve a thing."

"The local folks hate he singled you," Charlie said. "They're sending a committee to Kenyon's to convince him to fire that pair. They ain't any good except for trouble."

"Will that work?" I looked to my boss for the answer.

"It'll work if the others refuse to work roundup with them two. Kenyon will be forced to fire them. No way he can get his cattle up. It takes everyone and the cook now," Hainey said. "No, they'll be gone quickly when the committee tells Kenyon how it's going to be."

I figured if Kenyon fired them, that pair would think I was responsible and come looking for me like sore-toed bears. I'd face that when they came. A man could waste his whole life worrying about such trash that never happened. I was anxious to get on with roundup.

Daybreak found us trailing the saddle stock west into the basin country. Rice was bringing the supplies and food in his wagon. I rode drag—being the youngest and new man—and led the two horses loaded with our bedding. There was no problem herding them, for the horses were fresh as the cool morning wind, although they mixed with Brackett's, had a few fights, and sought their social places. Short was among them, and they soon learned to leave him alone. He was no leader, but Short liked his space, and with a few squealing, kicking fits he taught respect to the others. Brackett had a big brown Kentucky mare that took the lead. I figured she could outrun any of our mounts, but she proved to be a good leader, and we settled in for the ten-mile ride.

Sun time ten o'clock we joined up with the Rices' wagon, and the girls had their remuda to mix in with ours. I saw Ewell riding a big blue roan. On the wagon seat, Stout sat with her boots on the dashboard, her gloved hands holding the reins of a big team of draft horses. Tate and Erv waved at me from the horse herd. I pulled up and waited for them.

"Been to any good dances lately, H.B.?" the youngest Rice asked.

"A durn good one. I danced with three pretty girls all night long." I looked for Erv, but she was shaking her head in dismay at my story.

"Could they dance?" Tate asked.

"Tate, they could dance like Russian countesses. So light on their feet, why, it won't get no better waltzing with angels."

"You ain't going to no angel place, H.B. Bentley," Erv said as she rode up beside me. "You're going to hell for lying."

"I hate to hear you say that." I laughed as Erv

spurred her horse after one of the string that had broke from the herd.

There's folks in this world can sit a horse, but that Erv Rice could ride a snake to breakfast, I tell you. She was more a part of her mount than the saddle, and it was strapped down and not going anywhere. She reined him up and waited for us.

"You ain't as beat up as I thought you'd be," she said.

"You haven't looked that close," I teased, sharing a wink with Tate, who agreed with an "I know" nod.

Erv looked casually aside. "May never see it."

"Might not," I said, and booted the bay into a trot. "See you girls later."

"Come back when you can stay longer, H.B.," Tate said.

"Oh, for goodness' sake, why'd you say that to him?" Erv complained to her younger sister.

I twisted in the saddle and raised my hat to salute them. "I will next time." Tate waved, Erv merely looked aside. I wasn't impressing her all that much. But I'd figure a way to do that before this roundup was over.

"You doing herd duty or roundup?" Stout asked when I pulled alongside of her. Those girls did look better wearing their hats, I'd almost forgotten.

"Whatever Mr. Hainey wants from me."

"I'll put in for you and we'll get the breaks," Stout said, already figuring things out.

"Fine," I said, riding alongside her wheel. "How much further?"

"You can see the tree line. That's Fisher Creek. Nice place."

"Good," I said. "Of course, anything's good just so I don't have to farm."

"You been farming lately?" Stout asked.

"I was mowing and stacking alfalfa hay for a man down near Hayden's Mill all summer."

"You don't like farming, I take it." She expertly swung the team to avoid hitting a pothole with a wagon wheel and leaned her whole body over. Managed them better than any man.

"Hate it," I said. "I was sure glad I met Mr. Hainey and got this job." Stout nodded she understood.

"Tell me, did I insult Erv at the dance?"

"Lord, no. I guess not. Why?"

"She kinda acts like I'm poison today."

Stout laughed and slapped the mules with the lines to make them move out. "I can't help you. Erv's that way. But I'll bet you something."

"What's that?"

"She'll get glad quick as she got mad." Stout laughed at her own joke, and I short-loped off to catch up with the men. Ahead, I could see the line of cotton-woods and sycamores. Maybe Erv would act more friendly at noontime.

Noontime we were at the Fisher Creek camp. I took the iron stakes for the rope horse corral. With a big hammer, I drove the waist-high rods with the loop in the top into the ground. With rope strung through them, you had an instant fence. They were putting up a large canvas tent to use in case it rained. With the clear blue sky overhead I figured that was a waste of time, but one could never tell. I carried an oilskin slicker on my saddle, too, just in case. Beat having your butt soaked in one cold unexpected rainstorm.

The pen finished, I carried my hammer back up the short rise to the camp. I saw Erv building a fire and hanging kettles on the rack fit over it. I put the hammer in the toolbox, hiked up my chaps and jeans, and set to go by and talk to her.

"You the cook?" I asked.

"Yes, I am. Don't really like it, though. Sonny was the cook two years ago, but we made him horse guard after that. He ain't fussy enough for this bunch."

I grinned and shook my head. I wondered what the old cowboy had done wrong.

"He couldn't keep the shells out of the eggs and pancakes he cooked, for one thing. Said we were all too particular," she said, rising. "You can ride out and snake me in some wood. I'll need a lot of it for this bunch."

"Sure," I said, and went after my horse.

"She any better?" Stout asked me as I passed her girting up the bald-faced horse of theirs.

"Some."

"She'll get better. Give her some time."

"I will." I mounted up and rode off along the stream looking for some driftwood that was brought down by a flood. I tossed my rope over a tall limb stub and wrapped the rope on the horn. I clicked to the bay horse and he dug in. When the wood eased free he spooked a little and went off to camp at a high trot, him trying to see what was chasing him. The training would be good, so I bent way over, undid my loop, and rode after more. Stout joined me and we had races bringing in firewood, the tree parts or limbs barely hitting the ground behind us as we ran for camp. Baldy was quick, and I saw why they all rode him—he was a cat on his feet. I figured he could out-maneuver two other horses.

Sonny set off with the remuda. They wanted to save the standing feed up close to camp for the cattle we gathered. Tate was helping pack things from the wagon to the tent. They had a table set made up out of boards and benches to sit on. With the tent sides up it made a nice shady spot; with the sides down we'd have shelter.

I finally figured that if we used all that wood Stout and I'd brought in, we'd be there for years, and so we quit. I found an ax in the wagon box and began bust-ing it up. I'd done enough wood splitting for my mother, and I knew plenty about axes. This one was double-bitted and sharp, so the chips flew. Stout came and stacked it for me.

Brackett, Hainey, and Rice had ridden out to see how many head were close by.

"You don't like farming, huh?" Stout asked again, her arms full of wood. She stood waiting for my answer.

"I hate it!" I noticed a reflection like someone was using a mirror to signal. "There on the tent, see that?" I pointed to the bright circle on the tent cloth.

"What is it?" she asked.

"Don't you look that way, and just act natural like nothing's wrong. Someone has us under their field glasses."

"Why?" Stout asked. I saw Erv raise up from her Dutch oven and look my way.

"Damned if I know. But you think you know where they're located?"

"What do you mean, where they're hiding?"

"Yes," I said, hoping it was only an old telescope and not one of those long telescopic sights like I had seen on a sporting rifle. The hair on the back of my neck rose at the prospect. If it was a long-range rifle, they could pick us off like pigeons on a rafter.

"They must be up on that mountain south of here," Stout said.

"You mark the spot; I'm going up there after a while and see what they think they're doing." I busied myself with the ax and chopping to look normal as possible, but the hair on the back of my neck was hackled.

"Why would someone want to spy on us?" Stout asked, loading her arms with split wood.

"I can't say, but they may plan to take the herd away from us when we're done."

"Other words, scouting us out?"

"Maybe." I busted up more kindling. The one up there hadn't shot so far, so maybe my worst fears weren't grounded. Who knew? But I hated the notion someone was spying on us, obviously for no good reasons.

"How did you figure that was a telescope?" Erv asked when I brought her an armload of cooking wood.

"It's the only thing besides a mirror does that."

"I don't like it." She gave me a look of disapproval.

"I aim to put a stop to it."

Seated at the table, Erv peeled potatoes, the white clean ones stacked neat. They glistened as she rolled them deftly over her knife and separated the skin. "How are you going to do that?"

"Indian style," I assured her.

"Damn spooky. I wonder if the others seen it." Erv used the side of her hand with the knife to shield her eyes so she could look down the basin. There was no sign of the men.

I shrugged. I intended to ride up there and see if I could catch whoever it was.

"Stout, get your rifle out of the wagon box and put it on the table in the tent in case you need it." Enough was enough. Anyone decent would ride down to our camp and introduce themselves, not sit up there and leer at us through a spyglass.

"Where are you going?" Stout asked, blinking her eyes.

"I'm going to find out who's spying on us."

"I'll go too."

"No, you and Erv need to guard this place."

Stout didn't take orders. She jerked the .22 rifle out of the wagon and put it on the table. "Erv, use it if you need to. You know how." Then she stalked out and jerked the girth tight on Baldy. I took the Colt out of my saddlebags, stuck it in my belt, and waited for her. She reached in the wagon and drew out a well-oiled Winchester with a saddle loop and hooked it on the horn.

"Let's ride," she said, her eyes hard as diamonds.

"Just walk your horse till we make some cover," I said. "Then we ain't got as much distance to close in on them."

"You get killed, where do you want me to send your things?" Erv called out from her potato peeling.

"Oh, I got a brother in Silver City, New Mexico. His name's Atha."

"I'll be sure he gets them."

I shook my head. "She don't like our idea."

"Give her a day or two," Stout said to reassure me, and we trotted our horses toward the small stream.

On the far side of the creek under the canopy of the big trees, I nodded at her to go. We charged up the slope. The bay could run uphill or down, but Baldy, the horse Stout rode, could cut around those bushy junipers like a deer and never lose his stride. We were fast gaining the mountain, and I figured we'd scare hell out of whoever was up there. But I saw no movement, even when we stopped to let our horses blow. I stood up in the stirrups to survey the rest of the mountain. I couldn't see a thing moving.

"There goes someone." She pointed, and I saw the tail of a horse through the junipers lunging up the mountain high above us. The rider was less distinguishable, but he was quirting the fire out of his horse.

I set my rowels in the bay and we were off. I wanted

Stout to stay there, but there was no time to argue. Then I saw puffs of smoke and quickly realized they were pistol blasts intended for us. That worthless outfit was shooting at Stout and me.

"Give me that Winchester," I shouted above our horses' hooves shelling down the talus under their scrambling, saddle leather protesting.

She jerked the rifle free and swung the barrel to me. I took it and spurred the big horse on. When we reached the next flat I reined in the bay. The shot would be a long one, but when the rider cleared that next juniper up on the mountain, I intended to blast him.

With the buckhorn sight set on the front bead, I raised it up for distance. He burst into view and I squeezed off the trigger. The report of the bullet echoed and reechoed across the mountain face. His horse screamed and came over backwards. Stout and I watched helplessly as they tumbled over and over backwards down the mountain. The pained cries of the horse were the worst part. They were loud and drew chills on my skin. Half-sick, we looked at each other and then booted our horses uphill to where they landed.

The horse tried to rise but was bad hurt. He struggled to no avail. A careful bullet from my Colt ended his suffering, then his limp body slid several feet down the steep slope and lodged. Stout was off holding Baldy's reins and standing over the prone man. When I joined her I knew by his position he was dead.

"He ain't breathing, is he?" she asked as I listened for his heart.

There was blood on his vest. The .44-40 slug had found him, then he had pulled the horse over backwards. I was fast getting sick.

"You know him?" she asked, looking pale too.

I shook my head—I'd never seen him before. I couldn't contain it any longer and I retched. I grasped my knees and continued being sick. This swarthy-faced man, this outlaw, whoever I'd shot, that was the worst part. We didn't know why he spied on us or why he fled and shot at us. The vomit burned my nose and I couldn't stop the dry heaves.

"Who the hell is he?" Stout asked with big tears on her suntanned cheeks.

"Dammit, Stout, I don't know, but we can look on his person," I said, hoping the worst of my being sick was over.

"Oh, I ain't touching no corpse." She backed uphill two steps. "If he wasn't up to no good, then why did he shoot at us?"

"Stout, I don't know. Hell, woman, I don't know any more than you do."

"Sorry," she said softly. "I just wondered."

His pockets had five dollars in coins and a whorehouse token from a Tucson house of ill repute. Everyone had them; they were legal currency. I found a letter, too sweat-stained and worn to read. The envelope was worn fuzzy, but it was legible where it showed General Delivery, Flagstaff, Arizona Territory.

"I'll go check the saddlebags," I said, rising up. "Ain't nothing here says much."

"I never saw a man shot and killed before," she said, very subdued. The pallor under her suntan made her skin almost gray.

What could I say? I'd never shot anyone before either, and hoped I never had to again. My high bootheels teetered around in the rocks as I descended the steep slope to reach the horse's position. She followed. We were forced to crawl down backwards the last ten yards because of the steepness of the slide choked with loose rock where the horse ended up.

We finally reached the precarious spot beside the dead horse on the edge of the cliff. While I struggled to free the saddlebags the slide gave some and she clutched my arm. Staying perfectly still, we both inhaled and waited.

"Doing that jerking, you're going to cause us to go over that brink," she said, hurting my arm with her grip. I pried her fingers loose.

"Then get back up on the ledge so I can finish here," I ordered.

She sat firmly on her butt and chewed on her lip. "I can't."

"Why not?"

"Promise not to laugh?" Stout gave me a threatening look.

"I promise."

"I don't know why I even came down here." Then her expression turned to bewilderment; she kept glancing over the edge of the rock slide. The fall, I speculated, might be five hundred feet. We'd never survive it.

"Well, I didn't twist your arm to come down here," I complained.

"I'm afraid of high places," she managed to gush out.

"Stop looking down. That makes it worse. Turn around and start crawling uphill and off this slide."

"I will," she said, and closed her eyes. I could see the cold sweat running down her face. Stout wasn't kidding. I helped her turn around and get on her hands and knees.

"Keep crawling till you're back on the top ledge. It's wide enough up there to get your bearings. Go!"

She swallowed hard but never moved. I could see her body trembling, so I went with her or she'd never have moved. We crawled a few feet at a time. It seemed like an eternity. We managed to move only inches, then the loose rocks gave and we lost some of our gain. Her sharp inhalation marked the losses. My arm was on her waist to try and comfort her. I kept eyeing the ledge above, where our horses were ground-tied. More of the slide gave way. Rocks and debris clattered as they plummeted over the edge, bouncing off the face of the mountain and falling forever.

For a long minute I thought we'd slip back to the dead horse and off the mountain face to our certain death. Like a rug was being pulled from beneath us, the rocks slipped away and we scrambled to stay on the mountainside. Her cry caught in her throat. Finally we stopped sliding, then we made some real progress, and I gave her bottom a big final boost that spilled her facedown on the ledge. She bellied over with a quiet "Thank God."

From the effort to push her up on the ledge, I half turned and found myself on my back out of control going down the slide in a flush of loosened rocks toward the horse.

"H.B.!" she screamed, and I saw her terrified face above me. I finally landed at the dead horse, but he, too, had slid more. My heart was pounding in my throat. I felt weaker than I'd ever felt in my life, like I lacked the strength to save myself.

"Get a lariat!" I shouted at her. When she disappeared, I tried to crawl over the horse's legs and cut the saddlebags loose. A crunching sound began. The horse's body began to slip a few more inches down the slope. His limp head and neck were already hanging over the edge of the world. He must have shifted downhill six feet since I'd shot him and he'd first ended his descent.

"Damn," she swore. I looked up; the lariat was too short to reach me. "I'll get another," she said.

I found myself not daring to move for fear the whole field would go at the slightest change. Another small shift began, and several rocks below me fell off the face of the mountain forever before they struck anything below. I looked up for Stout's return and licked my dry lips. They tasted like alkali. This was one damn mess.

✖ 6 ✖

I never dreamed dying was going to smell so bad. I figured death would be tough, but the stink made the waiting a lot worse. Even a dead horse can pass gas. Seated only a foot away from his tail, I received the full force of such attacks his lower bowels released. Every second or so, the deep fill of crushed rocks under me shifted an inch or two further down without me even wiggling. As the deep layer of gravel ground its way downhill, it sounded like someone's clenched teeth being gritted together. Yet the sound was more than annoying to me, it was downright terrifying. I wondered how to escape my certain death. The horse's limp head and neck hung out in space and weaved a little when the slide moved. With each tremble of the ground the horse's corpse inched closer to falling through eternity. When it toppled off the cliff's face I figured I'd go in the rush too.

I wondered about Atha, my brother. He'd be shocked when he received my last effects. Though what the hell Erv would send him was beyond me. My throat felt constricted, and breathing became harder. I'd told Stout not to look down, but there wasn't any other place for me to look. If I'd been a buzzard up there, I could have spread my wings and floated for hours without a single wing flap. It was a long, long ways down to the bottom. I wanted to scratch my neck, but I didn't dare move. The crunch of rock against rock began again, and the horse and I slid a little more.

"Ease into the loop!" Stout called out from above.

Damn, she had tied enough ropes together to reach me. I turned and saw the lariat uncoiling at me. Thank God! The rope fell a few feet to my right. Should I lunge for it? Any movement at all would send the dead horse and me off the mountain into a final fall.

"Stay there," she ordered, and began to whip the rope to get it closer to me.

Beneath my butt I felt the slide begin to give way. My hand reached for the rope. The trickle of rocks off the edge became faster and faster. I lunged for the loop, and at that moment the horse flew away. Dust boiled up. I clung to the lariat with both hands as tons of rock began to plummet away in earnest. Like a great waterfall, the stream of debris spilled a thousand feet downward in a billowing cloud of dust. More rock slides went off under my scrambling boot soles as I dangled on the rope.

"H.B.! You all right?" she screamed.

"Yes, pull me up!"

"I'm trying."

Oh damn, the lariat wasn't tied to a saddle horn, she was holding the rope herself. Why in the hell I did it, I'll never know, but I had to look at the basin far below. The tiny tent and the wagon were barely a dot. My arms were about to be pulled from the sockets and I swung free in midair. I finally managed to get a toehold on an outcropping with my boot and took some of the strain of my weight off her. The muscles in my left leg trembled as my toe pressed down on the firm outcropping.

Then, using toeholds and small ledges, I began to work my way up the face of the mountain. Pausing to catch my short breath and rest my weary arms, I hoped Stout had the strength to last long enough for me to belly over the ledge.

"I'm coming, Stout," I said, still unable to see her, but knowing that she was the anchor to my life. I regrasped the rope and rested. Sweat was pouring down my face. The hemp was burning my palms, but compared to the alternative, it wasn't bad. My breath came in gulps and I resumed climbing.

At last I bellied over the ledge I had boosted her over. My upper torso safe, I collapsed facedown.

"Oh, thank God, H.B.," she sighed, and dropped to her bottom about five feet from me, the limp rope between us like an umbilical cord. I wiggled until I was finally on the ledge and then crawled over to her.

"You're wonderful!" I said. Then I kissed her, on the forehead, the cheeks, and her mouth. She looked at me in shock and disbelief. Finally I sat back up on my legs, took off my hat, and looked up at the pale blue sky and thanked God.

"I don't think I can get up," she said as I struggled to my feet.

"Yes, you can. We made it, gal. That was too close," I said, and tried to straighten out my achy muscle-cramping legs. She took my hand, and I pulled her to her feet.

"What now?"

"Load that dead jasper up and take him to camp. Maybe one of them knows him."

"How are we taking him back?" she asked hesitantly.

"Belly-down, I guess."

She grew very quiet. I glanced at her and then stopped. Her face was pale as a sheet.

"What's the matter?"

"I've never handled a dead man."

"I'll do it. Come on, we'll put him on Baldy, and you can ride double with me."

"Good," she said, and untracked like she was totally relieved. "I'll get the horses."

No one ever gets ready to handle a dead body unless you're an undertaker. They must get used to doing it so much. Gingerly I rolled the limp corpse inside my slicker so I didn't have to look at him or his form, then struggled to put him across the seat of her saddle. I roped him down on Baldy, grateful when that grisly job was completed. I mounted the bay, and she handed me the reins to Baldy. I let her use the left stirrup, and she swung up behind me. We left for camp. The ride down was much slower than our wild chase uphill.

"Who was he and why did he shoot at us?" she asked, holding herself respectfully back, which was hard on the steep parts. Several times she was tossed forward despite her efforts, and her form was pressed against my back. For a moment she clung to me, then righted herself. I almost forgot about the corpse across the bald-face horse. But not actually—the notion I'd shot someone needled me more than I wanted to admit.

"Damned if I know. Maybe he was just watching the Rice sisters through his spyglass."

Stout slapped my upper arm in contempt. "He won't have seen nothing."

"Can't never tell," I said, and went to singing my favorite cowherder song.

> Ol' Blue was a steer,
> The cowboys held dear,
> He saved them one dark stormy night.
> His head he tossed,
> And headed them out all right.
>
> Hi lo, hi la,
> We'll see him again someday.
> To the Triple C,
> He'll always be,
> A cowboy's dream come true.

He swam the Big Red,
His longhorns ahead,
The others close behind.
This great lead steer,
Who knew no fear,
Ol' Blue was one of a kind.

When they headed north,
He'd steer their course,
A-working for the boss.
There was always one more day,
Blue sure earned his hay,
With one more river to cross.

One girl loved Ol' Blue,
Her name was Lou,
She lived on the Triple C.
It broke her heart,
When they had to part,
But she knew Ol' Blue was free.

"Whose song is that?" Stout asked.

"Just an old night herder song I sing to cows, must
be a hundred verses to it. However, some of them
ain't for mixed company."

"I'm glad you spared me those. It's a nice song. I'd
like to learn the verses you sang. One more thing,
H.B.—I won't never mention you kissing me up there
if you won't," she finally said.

"Stout Rice, I'd have probably kissed old Sonny
Pitts if he'd saved my life."

"Ugh," she growled. "I'll never save him if that's all that men can think to do for thanks. You promise to forget it happened?"

"Sure, I won't say a word about it. Say, we'll practice that song together sometime, if you like. I've got some more parts we can sing." I went back to singing "Ol' Blue, the Lead Steer." Bet I was the first guy that had ever kissed her. Well, I was grateful to her, and I'd have done it over. But she was right, old Sonny with his five-day white beard stubble, no teeth, and his lip smeared with chewing tobacco juices might be more than a grateful person could stand to kiss.

"What's so damn funny?" she demanded, gouging me in the kidney with her thumb.

"Thinking about you kissing Sonny."

She pummeled my shoulders and back with the sides of her fists. "I ain't kissing no one, H.B. Bentley."

Forced to duck forward to escape her wrath, I could hardly contain my laughter. "I won't mention it, I promise."

"Good!"

I spurred the bay harder, and he jumped down a steep portion of the trail. The move threw Stout against my back again and forced her arms to encircle me to prevent her falling off. I half smiled while she wiggled against me to right herself.

She sputtered how I'd done it on purpose.

"Never." The bay horse kept picking his way off the steep mountainside.

Tate came riding hard to meet us when we came

down the final slope to the creek. A questioning frown darkened her eyes when she spotted the wrapped corpse; she reined up short.

"Who's dead?" Tate asked. "We heard shots."

"We don't know the jasper," I said. "He just started shooting at us, so I shot back." My answer seemed to satisfy Tate, and we went on to camp.

Brackett, Rice, and Mr. Hainey rode in the same time we arrived. They dismounted and hurried over to examine the shrouded body on Baldy.

"Who is he?" Hainey asked.

"Damned if I know. He was spotting us with a spy-glass. So Stout and I tried to ride him down and find out his business. He went to shooting at us, and I returned fire."

"That's the gist of it," Stout said, "except this guy's dead horse was on a slide, and H.B. went to find his things and nearly went off the mountain with the horse."

"Find anything?" Hainey asked me directly.

"No, sir, I never was able to get his bags off the horse. I was going to ride over later and see if there was anything left after the fall."

Ewell Rice and Brackett had the man laid on his back and exposed to the sunshine. They both were squatted on their bootheels, studying him hard. The man's face looked bluer than when I loaded him. I hated to even look at him.

"Recognize him?" Hainey asked the pair.

"I've seen him before, but can't figure out where," Rice said, pinching his whiskered chin and shaking his head ruefully. "Strange he'd pick a fight over just spying on us."

"There may have been more to it. Good men have been shot over nothing we know about. They were always singled out with no one around," Brackett said.

"That's a point," Hainey agreed. He searched the dead man's pockets.

"I've already took his money out. There wasn't much. Five dollars and a token," I said, handing the money to Ewell to examine. "I figured I'd find more in his saddlebags, but they went off in the avalanche with his horse."

Hainey straightened. "Looks like self-defense to me."

"Sure," Brackett said quickly.

Ewell Rice nodded in agreement and handed the money back to me.

"I say we bury him and go on. The law from Prescott would be two weeks getting here, and they wouldn't do nothing but take up time."

"Amen," Brackett said. "They ain't solved any murders or the rustling in this country either."

"Tate," Hainey said. "You go relieve Sonny and send him in here. Maybe he knows this dead man."

"Yes, sir," she said, and rushed off to her horse as if relieved to flee the situation. Both Stout and Erv were back by the tent and talking in low tones. The lines of worry creased their smooth brows when they looked in our direction, and they showed an obvious uneasiness toward the dead man.

"No one else around?" Hainey asked me.

"Just him, sir. He shot at us first."

Hainey's hand clapped my shoulder. "H.B., I'm sorry to drag you into this problem, but we're all in it with you. Everyone pairs up from now on. And, Ewell, you better arm those girls."

"They can shoot good as any man," Ewell said, like that was settled.

"Let's hope to God they don't have to," Hainey added.

"Where will we bury him?" I asked, anxious to have him in the ground and maybe out of my thoughts. "I'll get a shovel."

"I'll help. Ground is softer near the creek. Myself, I'd rather be buried under the trees; guess he would too," Brackett said, and walked with me to the wagon after a shovel for himself.

What were the dead man's wishes? I didn't know. It seemed my responsibility to lay him away since I'd shot him. The whole thing seemed very senseless. I could have been dead at his hands on the mountain, or even Stout. What in hell was he doing up there, and why did he run? I raised up and looked at the mountain for the answer, but there was nothing but bluffs and junipers dotting the slope.

Hainey produced a Bible from his things. The thin pages ruffled in the wind as he studied the verse he wanted. A Christian burial for a stranger seemed easy enough. . . . *Into the valley of death* . . . I shoveled out the sandy dirt mixed with stones. Then Brackett took his turn as the hole became deeper. I kept looking for Sonny to return. But there was no sign of the man.

Hainey even took to squinting his eyes and looking in the direction Tate had gone. There wasn't much to say. Ewell had gone to see if he could locate the dead horse and saddlebags, but I feared they were under tons of fresh rock and debris, judging from the magnitude of the slide.

The hole was deep enough. Not six feet but a respectable four feet, more than many men received.

"Sonny may never get back here," Hainey said in disgust, and opened the Bible. He began to read from Psalms. Near the end we all looked up at the approach of a horse. Sonny slid off his saddle and came limping along to the grave site. He spit a brown cud of tobacco to the side and looked down at the deceased.

"Know him?" Hainey asked, standing beside Sonny and leaning over to look down with him.

"Sure do."

"Who is he?"

"Buster Kimes."

"You sure?" Hainey asked.

"I seen him several times." Sonny punctuated his long speech with another large spit. "Must be a reward on him for a thousand dollars."

"Dead or alive?" Hainey asked.

"Yup, they'll pay it either way."

"What the hell is Buster Kimes doing out here?"

"Playing dead now. Damned if I know, Mr. Hainey." And Sonny spit again.

I was looking up at the mountain. I'd shot a real outlaw, some bad guy with a reward on his head. A thousand dollars was a lot of money. How did you collect a reward when the dead man was buried? Even for the money, though, next time I'd probably try to hold my temper and not shoot him.

"It sounds to me like you're going to be a rich man, H.B.," Mr. Hainey said, breaking my train of thought. "Oh, yes, let's finish this. May Buster Kimes rest in peace. Amen."

❖ 7 ❖

The next morning Mr. Hainey sent Stout and me up in the Breaks to bring in the cattle while the others fanned out to gather from the four winds. I'd picked the dun horse to ride.

I knew when I swung my leg over the saddle he'd break in two. He bogged his head and bucked once around the camp before I finally managed to saw his head up. He sort of gave in and acted like I'd ridden the silliness out of him. Stout rode up beside me on a big gray horse with a head as long as his body, but he looked powerful. I hated to ride ugly horses, but I didn't have to ride him.

"You've never been in the Breaks?" she asked as we crossed Fisher Creek and rode around the mountain's base. I considered the events of the day before. The dead man's horse had been buried in the avalanche, and Ewell came back from his search empty-handed.

Mr. Hainey had promised he'd help me collect the reward when we took the sell cattle to Flagstaff.

"Nope, I never been anywhere up here," I said, wondering why her middle sister had been so cold toward me at breakfast. Erv had taken an extra measure of avoiding me.

"Erv sure ain't getting any friendlier to me," I said to test the water. I was riding a few feet behind her and looked up to study her reaction.

"I told you she was like that. But she'll come around."

"Guess she must fancy some other guy up here." I waited to see what Stout would say.

She turned in the saddle and shook her head. "No, Erv ain't got a feller."

I booted the dun up beside her. "Will you put in a good word for me?"

Stout shrugged and then nodded she'd heard me, but she never promised a damn thing. We rode a long ways in silence.

"What are you going to do with the reward money?" she asked.

"I'd like to buy some cattle of my own, if there really is any money."

"Paw says there is."

"Well, I ain't got my hopes up too high about collecting it. That may be harder than anything. Them bounty hunters saw off those guys' heads and bring them back inside a tow sack. I seen one in New Mexico ride up and dump it out at a sheriff's feet."

"Ugh!" She made a distasteful face.

"I ain't too sure I'd come back up and dig him up for the money."

"Be tough," she agreed. "Don't ask me to help you."

I felt the dun horse gather up and halfway expected him to buck. Instead he spooked sideways at a cottontail that burst out of a patch of sagebrush. He wasn't totally through with his foolishness.

The Breaks were all she said about them, a maze of canyons and ridges. We cut cow tracks midmorning and split up to find them. I rode up a long hogback looking off in the junipers that forested the slopes on both sides. A cow bawled to her calf, and the sound brought a smile to my face. I drove the dun downhill and soon had a dozen she-stock, calves, and yearlings headed down the dry wash for the basin.

Bunching them up, I called it. You start gathering and put them in a bunch and go back for more until you have a good-size herd to take in. I looked up and saw Stout waving a lariat and hollering to her stragglers. Nearly thirty head were down in the open.

"They'll stay here," she said, grinning at me. "We're going to trail in a big bunch this evening."

I agreed and we rode off again in separate directions. These were mainly roan cows and calves, some with white faces, while others showed the old longhorn blood. One old brown cow had such long horns, she carried her head low, but she had a good late calf trailing her.

Past noon by sun time, I added a dozen more cattle to the bunch. Erv had sent cold corn cakes along with us for lunch. I slowly ate one and waited for Stout. It was a very uneventful, warm early fall day. We had enough cattle and needed to head them in. These cows weren't bad to drive. I hated dumb long yearlings by themselves; they never knew where to go except run away.

I looked up. Stout's voice echoed in the canyons as she brought more cattle down ahead of herself. In this group two Hereford bulls with Hainey's brand were bellowing at each other. They challenged one another several times and pushed each other around over some cow in heat. I rode out on the dun and split them up.

She came in and stopped her gray. "You see anyone?" Stout looked around like she was on edge about something.

"No," I said, busy eating the second corn dodger from my saddlebags.

"All day I've felt there's been someone watching me," she said, twisting in the saddle to survey the hills.

"See any flashing light like yesterday?"

"No," Stout said, but she still acted like something was amiss.

"You're just getting gun-shy," I said, and took a swig of warm water from my canteen.

"Maybe, maybe not," she said, looking hard over the hills behind us.

"Let's ship these sisters and their brood to camp. We've had a good day."

"Yes we have. We've found several head today,

H.B. In times past I've rode a week before and never gathered this many head together."

"Good. I want Mr. Hainey to keep needing me after roundup. He kinda talked like that in Phoenix this summer."

"He could do worse," she said, kind of snooty.

"Thanks," I said with a hard shake of my head. I'd never understand women. I kinda thought she'd say, well, something nicer than that.

Cattle on the move, we fell in behind them and went for camp, dust boiling, a few cows holding back till I busted them with my rope. Stout kept them bunched, and a crooked-horn roan cow took the lead, headed north like she knew the way. I was grateful for her actions. I took the drag.

We crossed Fisher Creek, and Stout fell in beside me. The trail dust streaked her face and places under her ear, and there was a muddy stripe on her cheek.

"You ever been married, H.B.?"

"*Me?* Lord no, Stout. Whatever gave you that notion?"

"Just wondered," she said, and spurred her gray away.

What did that girl have on her mind? I was forced to go to work because the cattle wanted to split and go back. Stout would make a good wife for some old boys I knew. For a woman she was tough as any man. But for my likes, she was a little too broad-made to appeal to me. I really had my eyes set on Erv. When Erv turned while fixing food or serving it and the dress swirled around her slender hips, my gut felt empty. Somehow I was going to impress her.

"How many?" Hainey asked me as he rode up with a stub of a pencil tucked behind his ear and the dog-eared logbook resting on his saddle horn.

"Twenty-eight cows, twenty-two calves and fifteen yearlings, two bulls with your brand."

"You two had a good day," he said, searching the cattle from his place as we let them scatter on the flat. "Many more up there?"

"Mr. Hainey, ask Stout. She knows that country."

Stout shoved the hat off her head so the rawhide string caught at her throat and the hat lay on her back. "There's several more up there, but the others will be tougher to get out." She shared a confident look with me.

Hainey nodded. "Good job, you two."

"Want us to go back tomorrow?" Stout asked.

Hainey nodded, and we left him to go find some grub. The dodgers didn't stick to my insides long enough.

Under the tent, we washed up, and Stout headed for the steaming kettle, me on her heels savoring the aroma of the stew, which made my mouth water.

"We found Hainey's old brown cow," Stout said to her sister, busy dishing steaming stew in a tin plate.

"Oh," Erv said.

"She's getting old. She used to hide from us up those canyons when you rode through, then she'd double back."

"She must be fifteen or more," Erv said.

I listened to the girls talk. I could hear a slight sound of envy in Erv's voice. Maybe there was a way I could get Stout to cook a day and have Erv all day to myself. What for, I wasn't sure; Erv certainly didn't even act like I existed.

"There's crackers on the table," Erv said, drying her hands on her apron when I went by with my plate.

"Thanks. You know that country up there in the Breaks?" I asked, hoping to start a conversation—or anything.

"Like the back of my hand," Erv said, and sat down on the bench across from me.

"Got any tips for a greenhorn?" I asked.

Erv shook her head and grew silent. I couldn't figure a damn thing else to say. I knew she disliked being confined to camp cook chores. She wasn't at ease in my company, and I didn't know what to do about it.

"Tell him about Mr. Sutter," Stout said with a big grin between spoons of stew.

"Who's he?" I looked at Stout, then at Erv.

"A man Mr. Hainey hired to help him last year," Erv said.

"Oh."

"He said he come from Nevada and had cowboyed a lot," Erv said. "The first day he rode in and quit. We were right here in camp when he threw his hat down and said he was leaving."

"What was wrong?"

"Sutter said there were too many rocks, too much

cactus, and the cows were too ornery. Said he was going back to Nevada."

"Mr. Hainey asked him if he milked cows for that outfit in Nevada. Sutter left in a huff."

"I haven't seen any ornery cows yet." I paused between spoonfuls.

"You will. The easy ones come out today," Stout said, rising up with her bowl for more. "Good food, sister, very good! You may get plumb domesticated with this roundup-cooking business."

Erv made a mean face at her older sister's back. It amused me.

"Who cooks at home?" I asked.

"We take turns. Whoever wins the horse race gets to watch the other two make the meal and wash dishes."

"When's the race?" I asked.

"There ain't one up here." Erv looked down, disgusted. "We do it at home coming back from chores. I'd race her in a country minute over who wears this damn apron, 'cause I can beat her at horse racing. She can't outrun me on foot either."

I looked over at her. Erv was definitely the prettiest Rice sister and the hardest-spoken one. Couldn't have everything, I guess.

"How many days will it take to get all the cattle worked?" I asked.

"A week to ten days; we'll have to work them here and in the north country, then we'll join the others for the drive to Flag."

"I guess we won't get back for the dance this Saturday?" I asked, wondering if I'd have another chance to dance with her.

"I don't know about you, but come Saturday I'm going to Pecan School House, and this bunch can come along or starve."

I almost laughed at Erv's determination, but instead I went to eating her rich stew. Maybe at the dance I could impress her. Nothing comes easy in life. My daddy always said nothing easy was worth a damn anyway.

Sunup the next morning was a soft gray promise in the east when I stumbled down to the pen to get my horse for the day. I noticed that Erv was there in her riding getup and no apron.

"Whistler," Erv said, and glanced at me.

"You win the race?" I asked, half-asleep.

"Nope, Stout's under the weather and I'm taking her place. You mind?"

"No, ma'am." I drew a deep breath, straightened my shoulders, and shouted, "Short," to Charlie Brackett, who was roping mounts out of the remuda for us.

I led my ornery horse away with the lariat handed to me and brushed off his back. Where I stood I had a good view of Erv as she saddled her horse. Pads, saddle, bridle. I let the reins trail. Finished with my own saddling, Short stood ground-tied. I fell in behind Erv and headed for breakfast, wondering how this day would turn out. My senses said slow down, but I was about to have a nervous runaway. This was my chance to impress the middle Rice sister. Lordy, I needed lots of help!

"That horse you brought surefooted?" Ewell asked over his plate of cakes and sweetener.

"He's that if he's anything," I said, wondering why he was worrying about me.

"Lot of them flatland cow ponies ain't worth a damn in the hills."

"Short's a mountain horse," I said, and took the molasses from Erv.

"H.B. roped that big bay with him," Mr. Hainey said in my defense. "Why you worried?"

"H.B.'s horse got a mean eye about him," Ewell said. "He looks like he'd break in two when he had a man in a tight spot. I don't like horses like that."

"He's all I've got," I said. "He does have fits, but I handle him."

"No offense," Ewell said, and dismissed his thinking away with a wave of his fork.

I understood his concern; riders counted on each other at times during roundup, and an undependable horse could sure mess up things. For the past two years Short was all I'd had for transportation. Good or bad, I did the best I could with him.

The Breaks looked unchanged. Erv led us as we rode single file in silence up the cow trail. She seemed very intent.

"Stout very sick?" I asked, since her older sister hadn't shown her face that morning.

"Naw, she'll be okay," Erv said.

"She was fine yesterday," I said.

"Two days she'll be fine."

"Sick to her stomach?" I really wasn't getting much out of Erv. Stout had acted perfectly well the day before.

Erv turned and with an "oh hell" scowl for me, shook her head. "She's having female times, for crying out loud. Let's drop it."

My face turned beet red. How the hell was I supposed to know? Me worried about her and getting all these evasive answers. Damn, I wanted to ride old Short over the next mountain and beyond.

"Are we going to split up at the spring?" she asked.

"Never made it that far yesterday; your sister Stout said it was up that canyon." I pointed to the south and the high cliffs.

Erv agreed with a nod and punched her horse on. The canyon walls grew deeper, and the signs of cattle more scarce. All the droppings I saw looked very old, but we rode up the sandy wash bed anyway.

We rounded the corner, and a few two-year-old steers stuck their tails over their backs and ran off.

Erv looked at me with a frown. "What's made them so damn wild?"

"Someone else has been chasing them to death." I stood in my stirrups to see where they ran to.

"What makes you think that?"

"Cattle ain't fools. You chase them much, they get so they run off when they see you coming."

"But who in the Sam Hill would run cattle up here?" Erv demanded.

"Hold up," I said, and rode over to inspect some-

91

thing on the ground. There was a ring of charcoal left from a fire. I dismounted, then carefully scanned the hills around us.

"What's that?" Erv asked, leaning over in the saddle.

"A fire ring, and it's not a day or two old."

"Who was camping up here?"

"Get off your horse and start looking. Someone has wiped the whole area clean with a branch. They had been doing something in this canyon besides camping, and they didn't want someone else to read their signs." I scanned the tops of the walls, wondering if we were being watched.

"Like what?" Erv asked.

"Maybe blotching brands. We need to capture those two yearlings we jumped back down the trail and check their brands. I'll bet they're blotched."

"You sure?"

"I'm not sure of anything, but there's something wrong here," I said, crushing the charcoal in my hand and standing up. "This fire is a couple days old."

"Two days old," she agreed, leading her horse and walking around the perimeter of the open spot. "That was the day we came and set up camp."

"Are you thinking what I am? Buster Kimes may have been the lookout for this bunch. That makes more sense than anything we know so far."

Erv nodded. But she had become quiet again like she thought they were still close. I tried to dismiss the notion they were even in the country.

"They ain't still around. Don't worry, they made

tracks when the shooting started the other day, I'd bet. Ride around and look for more signs."

"Come and look over here," she said.

"What is it?" I asked, hurrying to where she had stopped.

Under a sagebrush was what I suspected they had used to blotch brands—a cinch ring with a green limb bent through it for a handle. In their haste they lost it or it became too hot to handle, so they left it.

I tied it on my saddle with the leathers by the swells. "Mount up, Erv, we need to make circles till we find their tracks."

"What then?"

"I'll track them, and you can go get the others."

A worried look written on her face, Erv acted uncertain about my plans. "I ain't sure Mr. Hainey or Paw would want you to do that alone."

"That's what we'll do," I said, and booted Short out in the low sagebrush searching for signs of their horses.

We must have ridden around for a half hour, and I decided from the prints I found they'd headed southeast. The tracks were plain enough, three riders.

"Erv, you be careful and ride like blazes. I'll leave some sign to follow me by, like broken branches or three rocks."

"What are you going to do against a band of rustlers?" she demanded.

"Nothing foolish."

She looked at me hard. "I think we either both should go or both go back."

"Erv, please let me find how far they've gone. I'll wait for you all to come before I jump them."

"You won't do nothing foolish by yourself?"

"I won't. I promise. Now, get going."

Erv gave me a last long look, then slapped Whistler with the reins and headed back. After her "hee-yeah's" to her horse and the clatter of his shod hooves, she was gone. I sent Short off on the dim trail. I'd be lucky to keep on their tracks in the rocks, but in this tough country, there weren't many ways to go even if you wanted to hide.

Noontime I found myself high in the pines. They had done nothing to disguise their trails as they rode on. They'd drifted down the mountainside back into the thick juniper and piñons. I pulled up Short and listened. Nothing. No smell of campfire; they must be miles ahead. I rode into a narrow grassy clearing and spotted a low-walled cabin in the far end. I reined up Short and studied the situation. There was no smoke, nor movement around the building.

A horse nickered and old Short never answered, which I was proud of. It must be their camp, I decided. My heart ran much faster and I dried my sweaty palms on my britches. I kept Short almost in the brush as I rode closer. If I needed, I wanted to be able to cut back in the evergreens for cover should I come under fire.

"Raise your hands," someone ordered.

My heart pounding in my throat, I knew my days were numbered. The unseen man rode his horse out of the towering stand of juniper behind me. I still couldn't see him.

"Keep them hands high," he reiterated firmly. "Where's your gun?"

"In my belt," I said, feeling cold, clammy sweat run down my ribs under my vest.

"Don't move," he said, and pushed his horse in close.

Too close for Short. He went to kicking at man and horse. The man shouted. I whirled to see him go off his horse on the far side to avoid Short's flying heels. His pistol harmlessly discharged into the air, which crowded his spooked horse into Short.

I went to screaming at Short to go. He bolted out so hard, he almost unseated me, but I found my seat in the saddle as he tore off down the meadow at breakneck speed. My only problem was Short was headed directly for the cabin, and two more figures had come out with rifles. There was no reining Short aside. I drew out the Colt from my belt and began to shoot over his ears, which only doubled his speed directly at them.

The puffs of smoke from their rifles meant bullets. I figured their hot lead would soon find Short or me and we'd be dead. But my return fire sent them hastily inside; we swept by the cabin with them trying to shoot at us out the windows. I kept low in the saddle and booted that crazy horse of mine into the sparse timber for cover.

Short crashed into their picket line of horses. I whipped out my jackknife as the horses crowded away from Short. I cut ropes and drove the half dozen ponies ahead of me down the mountain.

"He's getting our gawdamn horses!" someone shouted back by the cabin. I could hear the sound of bootheels hitting the ground as they came through the thin pines toward me. I didn't have time for more. I spurred Short on, even though I lacked cutting two of their horses loose. Waving my arms and shouting for the freed horses to go, we went down off the hillside in a stampede.

The men shot after me. But their efforts to stop me did them little good, for I was well out of pistol range, and the thin young trees on the slope covered my retreat. Short was headed down the steep mountain, and most of their saddle stock was too.

In the canyon, I drew up Short to let him breathe and reloaded my Colt with shells from the carton in my saddlebags. The old .31 rimfire wasn't the greatest pistol made, but it slung lead, and usually that's all that counted. My smaller-caliber revolver would kill someone as fast as a .44, only not leave that big a hole in their hide.

I decided to circle west and see if I could head off Hainey and the others. Those three gunslingers were more than I wanted to tackle by myself. Besides, they wouldn't get far on foot. I set Short west at a lope and I tried to remember points and familiar features of the mountain range to find my way back.

A good idea is to line up a mountain peak or formation and use it for a guide. Except when I topped out on the next ridge, in the north, the Mogollon Rim looked the same, a long blue towering line. At first I felt mildly confused, but still confident enough. I rode a ways further. The camp and Fisher Creek had to be north. All I needed to do to find them was go north and I'd meet up with Mr. Hainey and the others. After an hour or two more riding I discovered, with a sinking feeling in the pit of my stomach, one clear and simple thing: I was lost.

❈ 8 ❈

When sundown came in the shadowy deep canyon, I was leading Short and scuffing my pointed boot toes down the sandy dry wash. Nothing looked familiar. I had some old jerky left in my saddlebags. I paused to water Short at a stale hole with skimmer bugs flitting the stagnant surface. So he was fine. But I had no blankets, and night would be colder than the blue devil in the mountains. I decided to stop and make a fire. If I found enough dry wood before pitch dark, I'd probably stave off capturing pneumonia. This all was very stupid, for I should have crossed back into the right country and rode into camp by this time.

I wondered if they had gone after the outlaws, more of that bunch Buster Kimes must have belonged to, living up there and cutting out folks' cattle. They'd sure dance on a long rope if and when the ranchers caught them. I tied Short so he didn't wander and went to gathering sticks. The sun was gone and the owls were out hooting when I sat on my haunches and started the blaze. It would be a long night.

Mr. Hainey would go to figuring I wasn't very much of a hand, getting separated from my own outfit. If I couldn't find my way back, he didn't need me and I'd be back to cutting hay.

I wondered who the outlaws were. I tried to figure how I could identify them if I ran into them face-to-face in town. One was baldheaded—I saw his bare head snow white 'cause he wore a hat all the time to hide the fact. The guy who stopped me and went for my gun before Short kicked him off his horse had a mustache. I hoped I could pick him out of three other rustlers. Fear had a way of distorting what a fellow sees at times. I figured I was fully afraid the whole time with crazy Short running straight into their camp on a rampage. But if I hadn't scattered their horse stock, they might have caught me, and I'd be worse off than lost, pitching fine kindling on my fire.

Dawn peeked over the mountain like a flannel blanket. The temperature in the canyon was close to frost. My firewood was nearly spent, and I rubbed the circulation back in my arms under the slicker that helped to hold in the heat (but not much). I finally saddled Short and headed up the mountain above me. I sure wanted to find Fisher Creek and the camp before this day was over.

Noontime I reined up and listened. The narrow canyon we rode down was high-walled. There was a sound

I couldn't quite make out, but my ears strained to listen. I spurred Short and we raced down the loose, dry sandy wash bed. I rounded a bend and looked into Erv's shocked face.

"Thank God. You're alive!" she shouted, and dismounted to run and meet me.

We met each other and I hugged her. I swept her off her feet and swung her around. She was babbling like a fool, and I knew I was so damn glad to have her to hold. I stopped and looked down in her blue eyes. Then I kissed her on the lips real hard. I couldn't help myself.

She tasted like clover, Clover salve—a greasy rich menthol ointment that was sure to cure cracked teats on a milk cow, baby diaper rash, and saddle galls. The taste was very sobering. Erv froze. In disbelief she held the back of her hand to her mouth and stared at me.

"Did they catch the rustlers?" I asked.

"No, they were gone. But we figured they had killed you."

"What next?" I asked, enjoying holding her and not wanting to move.

"They sent Sonny to get the law over here quick as they can come."

"How long will that be?"

She looked into my eyes as if searching for something. "A week or more."

"Why, those guys will be in hell and gone by then." Dammit if she was going to stare up at me. Clover salve or not, I was going to kiss her again. I did.

When I released her after that, she took two unsteady steps back and looked shocked to death. "I can't do this," she said, retreating.

"Why not?" I demanded.

She shook her head. "I can't, I can't." Tears streaming from her eyes, she hurriedly mounted and started to ride off.

I swung up on Short, confused worse than the night before when I was lost. I followed her.

"Why can't you?" I demanded, riding on her horse's heels.

She glanced back and looked at me again in disbelief. "I just can't! Don't ever do that to me again, H.B. Bentley. Ever, ever again!"

What in the hell was so bad about me kissing her? I hadn't done nothing wrong or acted indecent. Those Rice sisters were crazy. I was fast getting in the same shape trying to figure them out. I fell silent and followed her northward out of the canyon.

We topped out, and beneath us the brown grassland invited us back. The camp, with the sun-cured brown tent pitched, sure looked like a homecoming. The sight of the grazing cattle spread across the familiar basin made me sigh deeply. Even the familiar green farm wagon made my return the best kind of homecoming I could ever remember.

Mr. Hainey rode out to shake my hand.

"Damn, H.B., we figured that you'd gone to Boot Hill somewhere out there."

"I tried to drive their horses off. Guess I didn't get enough of them gone."

"They got away before we got there. We found three head of their horses that had wandered back in the meadow. Saw the severed ropes. Guess that was your knife that cut their lead ropes?"

"Sure was."

The others came out with their coffee cups in hand. Stout gave me a big smile. I dropped off Short and took the cup that Charlie Brackett brought me. The coffee tasted good, and I was proud to see each one of them. Erv took Short to unsaddle him and told me to go on.

"Well, tell us what happened," Stout said, sitting herself across from me at the table.

I went to explaining. I tried to make Short's absolute runaway not so much his damned ironheadedness but my plan. I also acted like I was too far away and the country too tough to cover at night—I omitted the lost part, too. And after a lot of questions I finished with, "I was coming back the long way, I guess, when I run into Erv."

She was nowhere in sight. I wished she hadn't taken my kissing her so damn bad, but it certainly hadn't helped my case with her. I never expected Erv to ride off bawling her eyes out after I kissed her. She could have whipped me for taking advantage of her, but crying?

The law was coming from Prescott. They had found several steers the day before with made-over brands. But we had calves to work and brand.

Daybreak I felt the anxious excitement like everyone else mixed with the servings of coffee, eggs, ham, biscuit, and good company. There was an air in camp before the dawn that cow-working time brings out in folks that own and handle them. Branding and working cattle for cowboys is like the sacraments are to religious folks, a very serious, sacred time. When dark came that night we'd be too tired to remember much, but afterwards it would come back all year, the funny incidents and the wrecks. There would be wrecks, too, for working cattle was dangerous business. No one wanted anyone hurt, but that, too, was a part of the cow business.

I chose the bay and we went to work. Tate took the horse herd to grass. Stout, who seemed recovered from her "female illness," rode Baldy, Erv a blood bay; Ewell was on foot to brand and work the cattle with Charlie. Mr. Hainey keep the logbook sitting on a gray.

The sharp smell of the branding fire cut the cool air as the fiery sun began to rise. Hearing the bawl of the milling mama cows to their babies—I knew it was working time. A hand rode into the herd, picked out a calf, roped the calf's heels, and drug him to the fire.

At this point steers were made. The mountain oysters were removed from bull calves and pitched into the branding fire. They were heated till they split and made a popping sound like a .22. Then one of the men would dismount or run over to spear it on a jackknife, brush any dirt off, and eat it with a grin.

The Rice girls ignored our feast. Though as the day progressed, there was less effort by the men to find the treasure when one popped from the fire onto the ground nearby.

Branding, dehorning, and castration is hard work and ceases to be fun long before noontime. You and your horse sort of get in the groove and do it. Heel another calf and start for the fire. The smell of branding is one of breath-catching hair afire. A good brander knows the hair must be burned away so the hide looks like good saddle leather. Such a brand will mark that calf's side long as it lives. Any less will hair over and lead to arguments.

With three brands here to work, the three heelers, Erv, Stout, and I, had to shout out the brand of the critter's mama. That way it received a Quarter Circle Z, an R Bar T for the Rices, or Brackett's B Slash, and the ownership was resolved. We saved the maverick yearlings for last. They were to be split between the ranchers. Some were bulls, and I wasn't really fond of roping those strong devils. The chance was good of those stout critters getting both me and the bay jerked down. One or two were past two years old, and since they were brindle-colored on their Hereford hides, no one wanted them left bulls.

"The turned-down-horned one first," Stout said, and rode by me swinging her rope. I knew what she meant and jerked the bay around to follow her.

The yearling with thick, wide-set horns quickly realized what we were up to and headed for the mountain. Stout booted Baldy up beside him. Expertly Stout's rope sung through the air and settled around his hat rack. She turned her horse off to jerk the bull around.

I rode in for the heel catch. My loop wrapped around his hind feet, and when I jerked up he was trapped.

The bay scooted his hind feet under him, and we had the devil stretched between us. Our ropes taut on his head and hind legs, he went down making the last deep bass sounds that he'd make as a bull. His line of progeny would be stopped and he'd bear the new owner's brand.

The new steer protested when the branding iron was applied. Ewell stepped back and nodded at his work.

"Next time rope the damn things closer to the fire; the iron nearly got cold running over here," her father said, serious as hell, and started back to his fire.

Stout gave him a look to kill as she rode over and stepped off to undo the head catch from the steer's head. I backed the bay so the animal's hind feet were useless and he couldn't rise up and horn her. With her mounted I pitched the slack and my rope came off his feet. The critter had enough and wandered off without much anger left.

We went for the other big ones.

"He wants one in his lap," Stout said, turning in the saddle to give her father a peeved look. "Watch this!"

Stout charged a large unbranded heifer for the branding fire. She held back roping her, though, until she had Baldy in a good position. Ewell saw her coming and began to run. The rope in Stout's hand flashed and she tore off to the side, turning the heifer over hard on her flank, only a foot from the fire. Ewell ran over and sat on the heifer's head while Charlie tied her hind legs.

"You did that on purpose!" he shouted angrily after Stout. "Come close to getting us killed!"

Ewell couldn't see the smug look on Stout's face, but I did.

"I'll put this one in his lap, too," she said under her breath as we worked out the next maverick from the herd. I grinned to myself. Stout was no one to cross.

As the sun dipped low in the west we dropped out of our saddles, bone-tired as our spent horses that snorted wearily. It was over. We had worked eighty-seven calves, thirteen yearlings. There were fifty fat two-year-olds and seven cull cows to take in with us, but the numbers were proving disappointing. There weren't any more cattle left in the hills.

"We'll work the high country next week," Mr. Hainey said as we finished the branding. "That'll give these young folks a chance to go to the dance at Pecan."

"Good for you, Mr. Hainey," Stout said. "We was going to quit you anyway and go."

"I figured that." Hainey laughed, and then shook his head. "Damn, I hope we do better next week. Them rustlers may have cleaned us out."

"It worries me," Ewell said warily. "Almost wish H.B. hadn't scared them away. We might have learned where they sold them."

"One thing, H.B. found them, and none of us had. He sure saved me making a big mistake about them damn Mormons," Brackett said, and his words seemed to satisfy everyone.

I wasn't near that certain that those rustlers wouldn't be back, but if I had averted a range war between Charlie Brackett and the Mormons, I felt good. I looked at Erv, but she quickly looked away. Everything else was going so damn good for me, except I damn sure wasn't getting anywhere with Erv Rice.

I figured my chances of staying on with Mr. Hainey were looking bad unless more cattle showed up. His neighbors, they were accepting me as a hand even if the middle Rice girl was damn sure avoiding me.

The deputy arrived Saturday morning at the Hainey ranch—long-faced man, close-shaven, with a high-priced felt hat that he pushed back on his head with his thumb. He sat a long-necked, running-type black horse.

"Mr. Hainey around?" he asked, pulling the makings out of his tweed vest and rolling himself a cigarette one-handed. His nickel badge was pinned on his chest and shone in the midday sun.

"He's coming," I said. "My name's H.B."

The deputy never offered his moniker. Without a word he reined the black around and touched him with a spur. Sort of made me mad, so I went back to resetting a front shoe on Short. I heard Hainey say something to the man, but I didn't give a damn what the deputy did. If he was too uppity-acting to even give his name, he could ride his skinny heinie off looking for them rustlers without my help.

"Mr. Hainey says you shot the outlaw Buster Kimes?" the deputy asked.

I looked up as I finished the nails on Short's shoe and dropped the hoof.

"Sonny Pitts said that's who the man was."

"There's a reward."

"Good, how much?"

"Yarborough, this is H.B. Bentley," Hainey said, realizing the coldness between the two of us. I didn't owe this fancy lawman a damn thing.

"Yes," he said. "Kimes's reward, last I saw it, was five hundred. What do you know about Buster's operation?"

"He was spying on us. I wanted to know why. He shot at Stout Rice and me, so I shot back. Got lucky."

"Lucky, I guess you were. Kimes was a killer. He gunned down two deputies in St. John's."

"I shot him at long range with a .44-40. That's all. He was dead when we got to him. His things were buried with his horse in a rock slide."

"I'm certain the reward's five hundred for Kimes dead or alive."

I nodded. "What do I need to do to collect it?"

"I'll file a report if Mr. Hainey and some of the others will sign it. The money will be waiting for you over in Prescott with the sheriff in a few weeks."

"We're going to Flagstaff in a week with the cattle," I said, not wanting to have to traipse all over the world to collect my money.

"Then I'll have them send it to the law there for you to pick up."

We talked about the rustler camp. He cast a weary eye south, but he didn't look like a tracker or a man that liked to sleep in a bedroll. He appeared to me to be a pencil pusher who would fill out a report and go back to his office. Yarborough wrote it all down and said he'd tell the state brand inspectors to be watching for the cattle. I figured that was the last we'd hear about them or the crooks.

After Rosita's lunch, the deputy took his leave. I didn't bother to see him off. I left that to Mr. Hainey and went to saddle Short for the ride to the Pecan School House.

"Why were you and that deputy acting like bristled-up yard dogs?" Hainey asked as I finished saddling Short.

"He ain't going to do a thing about those rustlers." I was so mad, my breath was raging through my nose.

"You're probably right. But hey, that reward will be nice to pick up in Flag," Hainey reminded me.

"I'll believe it when I see it."

"Oh, you'll see it," he said as I swung up in the saddle. "Have a good time at the dance. Tell those girls not to dance you to death tonight."

"I won't be back until the morning. I'm staying for the storytelling tonight."

Hainey waved good-bye, and I set out. The reward money sounded good, but my chances of working for the man all winter wouldn't be much unless we found a lot more cattle on the upper ranges. Those rustlers had made a large haul, from the signs. Damn, they couldn't possibly evaporate those cattle. I was sure perplexed about the matter.

"It ain't your fault." Tate tried to cheer me up. We were eating dry cheese and cold biscuits on the tailgate of the Rice wagon. Long shadows were spread across the school yard.

"I see you brought your bedroll," Stout said.

"I didn't aim to miss a thing," I said, trying to liven up the conversation. "I just wish we could find those stolen cattle."

"It'll sure be slim pickings at our house this winter if we don't find more. I hope we find them in the hills."

"Be honest," Erv said, almost impatient. "We were in the high country a month ago, and those cattle ain't there. They were in the basin last spring. Those crooks stole them and they're gone."

I looked at her. She folded her arms and turned away. Erv had a bluntness about her that was downright deliberate.

"We can still hope," Tate said to her sister's back, making a face.

"Hope all you want, little sister. The Rices are near broke."

Stout shook her head to dismiss Erv's hard words. "We ain't broke, and we're better off than most people. We won't be buying any fancy horses or bulls this year, but we aren't going to starve either."

"That's easy for you to say." Erv stomped off toward the schoolhouse.

"Is she that upset at me?" I asked Stout.

"Some," Stout said. "But Tate and I will dance with you. Won't we, little sis?"

"We sure will. Till the rooster crows, if they fiddle that long." Tate locked her arm in mine and headed me toward the schoolhouse door.

"She'll get glad," Stout said, and caught up with us in a few strides.

I noticed that dark-eyed Mormon girl Darling Moore head through the schoolhouse doorway in the company of three or four boys in their late teens. Tate made a pensive set to her lips at the sight of Darling. Guess they were both in competition for that Texan Jason, who I had not heard nor seen that evening. But I did look around for him.

We joined Erv on the bench like it was the Rice homestead in the middle of the south wall. There were notches cut in the bench edges where someone who'd been bored had carved them. The cuts made no sense, so I sat down and ignored them.

The fiddles started and I danced with Tate. Erv had a case of the "I ain't looking at you" stares. They played the "Tennessee Waltz," and I remembered dancing with girls at home to it. Kansas girls danced like the Rice girls. Some were a lot heavier on their feet, but I guess the Rice sisters practiced at home a lot. I remembered them "one-and-two-counters" that watched my feet and were way behind the music.

"Would it hurt one thing if I danced with Jason Combs?" Tate asked.

I must have swallowed hard, for I never expected her to ask me.

"I don't know, Tate."

"It wouldn't hurt a bit. Of course, he may never ask me again," she said, sounding down.

"What about all those boys over on the north side?"

"Oh, they're Mormons and they won't ask me."

I swung her around. Those Mormon boys needed to see what they were missing. Why, when I was eighteen I'd've given a month's wages to have had a girl as graceful on her feet as Tate to dance with. And as pretty.

"Why not?" I asked under my breath.

"Hell, either Paw or Stout would run them off. You and Paw ran into each other the first day. You know how he is. I'll never forget it. He came stomping out of that store and told us Mr. Hainey had hired a gutsy kinda cowboy."

"What did Stout say after we met?"

" 'He may be gutsy, but he's clumsy too.' " We both laughed and danced away. "She didn't know you could dance."

I waltzed a set with Stout. We took a break for lemonade. After the sweet drink Stout shoved Erv at me to dance. Erv was so stiff starting off, I figured she'd shatter the first few minutes on the floor.

"We got off on the wrong foot," I said.

"My dancing?" she asked, almost stopping.

I shook my head and pushed her on. "No, I mean you and I."

"I don't know what you mean."

"I mean—" I lowered my voice "—kissing you up there."

She nodded sharply; the anger was still in her eyes. I was not gaining a damn thing, but I didn't intend for her to ruin my Saturday night.

"I can't believe you didn't have a war with that Texas bunch or a dang thing," Mr. Hainey said as he leaned on the corral while I unsaddled Short. "Must have been a plumb uneventful night."

I shrugged.

"You have a good time?"

"Good enough. I think this cattle rustling has taken the heart out of me and the Rice girls."

Hainey agreed with a bob of his head. "Work years building a herd, and some lazy no-accounts steal all your profit. They'll turn up. We'll need to ride more range and keep a better eye on our stock. Never lost this many before. Kinda like locking the gate after they stole the damn horse, though, ain't it?"

"I guess. Only thing was, I can't believe they got away with it."

"What do you mean, H.B.?"

"Those rustlers had to have someone help them. That many blotched brands, why, a brand inspector had to be blind to let them by with that many run-over brands."

"I know that business of how and where they'd sell them is our only hope. I keep thinking they may show up somewhere and we'll get word. Come on, Rosita's got supper on. Let's keep her in a good mood."

"I'm coming," I said, removing my hat and wiping my face on my sleeve. I sure wanted more answers. "Mr. Hainey, what are you going to do if we don't find those cattle?"

"Suck in my belt and go on."

I nodded and followed him to the back porch. Guess I had wanted him to say he couldn't use me this winter. Then I'd have that over with.

"You know," Hainey said as he finished washing and slowly dried his brown-spotted hands on the towel, "a man can get an ulcer worrying about things like this. I've made up my mind I ain't letting these losses ruin my life. Someday I may or I may not find those jaspers. If I do, I'll settle with them."

"I hope I can recognize them the next time I see them."

Hainey dismissed my concern with a simple head shake. Then he hung his hat on a peg and went on to the dining table. The food smelled mouth-watering; I was starved and didn't know it.

We met the Rices in the morning and headed up in the foothills. The wagon was forced to ford the same small stream six or seven times. The road was so narrow, I felt sorry for Stout being thrown all over the seat having to drive the boulder-strewn path.

I gathered up some cows and calves along the way and drove them behind the wagon. I'd been to happier funerals and wakes. Everyone was acting so glum, it hardly seemed like the same bunch. I even took a notion once that mowing alfalfa was more fun. Things were bad when I thought that about punching cows.

Brackett and Sonny rode in about midmorning from the east to join us. We were fixing to set up camp in a long meadow fenced in by the slopes of ponderosa pines. The air was cool, but the sun warmed me.

The others scattered out to search for cattle. I stayed to help Erv set up the tent and the corral. I was driving in tent stakes when up rode the two Texans—Jason and Dobe. I felt naked without my pistol, but as usual, the Colt was in my saddlebags.

"Hello," Erv said, shielding her eyes with the side of her hand to look at them.

"Ma'am, I guess you couldn't tell us if the boss of this outfit is hiring, but we're needing jobs," Jason said.

She shook her head. "We don't need no one. Rustlers about cleaned us out."

"I reckon I'll wait till someone of authority comes," Jason said, smart like, and dismounted. Dobe did too. "You going to offer us coffee?"

"I told you straight out. No one is hiring up here. Now, get out!"

"You're pretty brave, ain't you, gal?" Jason advanced on her. Erv retreated into her tent.

I came with the hammer in my hand, my belly full of his smart-ass ways. "You heard her. She invites who she wants to coffee." I stepped between her and Jason.

"Well, if it ain't H.B. Bentley." Jason looked me up and down.

I slammed him in the jaw with my left hand. He went sprawling out on the ground, and I quickly drew my fist back when Dobe made a threatening move.

"Get your partner on his horse and you ride out," I said. "We don't need your kind here."

Then I heard Erv click the lever-action .22 shut, and Dobe raised his eyebrows. She stepped beside me. Jason struggled to his feet, rubbing his jaw.

"I'll get even with you, H.B., for this, and when I do I'll kill you." His black eyes filled with hatred as he and Dobe retreated to their horses. I knew I still had to settle with him.

"Get out of here before I gutshoot you," Erv said.

We watched them ride away. I took the rifle by the barrel and moved it aside and looked at Erv. "You ever gutshot anyone?"

She shook her head and ducked away. I checked to be sure those two were actually leaving.

The cow gathering was uneventful. Short even forgot how to buck for the week. The shortfall in numbers of cattle we found in the high country became more obvious as the week drug on, and it became harder to hide the disappointment for the ranchers.

"Boys, we've survived worse," Hainey said to liven up the crew as we ate supper.

"I say we offer a reward," Ewell said, obviously angry at the turn of events.

"Who in the hell's got money to pay it?" Brackett asked.

We all smiled at each other. I'd offer them my reward money, but that was all the stake I had. Maybe I would do that before it was over, but I hadn't collected it yet either. It might be like the cattle—gone in thin air when I got to the law office in Flag.

Friday we had all the selling cattle bunched in a trap at Hainey's upper place. So Saturday afternoon I rode over to the Rices' and went to Pecan with them. My bedroll stowed in their wagon, I rode with Erv and Tate. We went ahead of the wagon and all the dust. They were tongue-tied silent.

"You girls sure have sullied up today," I complained as we rode. Stout was on our heels with a big team of blacks and the familiar green wagon.

"We're having a disagreement," Tate said.

"Tate's being bullheaded is all," Erv said.

I reined in the dun I'd borrowed to ride to the dance. "What is she bullheaded about?"

"She told us she was dancing with that damn troublemaking Texan Jason if he asks her tonight, and Stout and I said we'd whip her first."

"What would it hurt for Tate to dance with him?" I asked.

" 'Cause . . . why, he called you out. You'd let my

baby sister dance with a no-good damn fancy-Dan Texas devil?"

"What would it hurt?" I asked.

"Oh, for crying out loud, H.B. Bentley, you're the most stupid man I've ever known." Erv glared at me.

"Go for a ride, Tate," I said, glaring back at Erv.

"Remember you're on my side," Tate said, and spurred her horse away.

"H.B., how could you ever say that?" Erv reined her horse to a halt in the middle of the road.

"I say let her dance with that little cockerel. She'll never see how sorry he is till she knows him, and when she does she'll come to her senses."

"That's plumb stupid!" Erv's hard look was cold and mean as a panther.

"You two quit arguing and get out of my way!" Stout shouted at us as the team nearly ran over the top of us in the road.

We reined our horses to the side for her to go by, but we were locked in an impasse. Erv was boiling mad at me for my idea about letting Tate dance with the Texan. I was angry as hell she wouldn't listen to reason. I finally booted my horse and left her to sull. She was too bullheaded to even talk to.

Things went from bad to worse at the school yard. Stout joined in on Erv's side, and we verbally went two more rounds. There was no talking sense to those two, so I left them to stew and went for a walk. The Texans weren't in sight, and I figured all the arguing was probably for nothing. They might be out of the country, and that would be fine for me. I felt half-guilty arguing for them since they were so damn ill-mannered, but I'd seen the look in Tate's eyes, and they weren't that low in her notions. A large dose of bad medicine can cure you in a hurry.

"You're the new ranch hand works for Mr. Hainey?" a girl asked.

I stopped and removed my hat to stare into the round doe eyes of Darling Moore. She was the cutest thing I'd seen in a few roundups, and my legs felt weak standing there.

"Yes, ma'am. I ride for the Quarter Circle Z."

"Well, we only live about two miles down the North Cut from Mr. Hainey. Our brand's the M O," she said.

"We've been out on roundup. I'll remember that brand."

She wrinkled her small button nose at me. "Ah, all we've got is milk stock."

"I aim to have a ranch someday of my own."

"Tough business, isn't it?"

"Hard, but I may have a stake coming. We'll have to see." I felt very conspicuous standing there in the golden setting sun and talking to this short pretty girl I guessed to be eighteen or so.

"I'd be glad to dance with you, mister." She kinda twisted her waist half around and back while she waited for my answer.

"Why, sure, I'd be proud to dance with you." I swallowed hard, trying to think fast enough so she didn't get away. "Sorry, ma'am, I didn't introduce myself. My name's H.B. Bentley."

"Darling Moore." She drawled those words, and I had to draw in some extra air.

"You just call me H.B. and save me that dance," I said, and went on back to the Rice girls.

When I got there, they were dishing out beans they'd reheated for supper. I thought they'd scorched them, but I wasn't about to say a damn thing in the mood they were in, both Stout and Erv glaring at me. It was like they'd rode over sitting on a nail.

"We'll do the dishes later," Stout announced, and dumped her tin plate and spoon in the kettle of boiling water on the fire.

I heard the fiddles begin playing the "Shenandoah Waltz," the lilting two-step music drifting out in the yard. It was time to get inside and take our places. Still not speaking, we stood up and headed for the schoolhouse.

"How come Ewell ain't here?" I asked as we crossed the yard.

"He went to Humphries," Stout said under her breath.

"Where's that?" I asked, looking at them.

Stout took my shirt sleeve and pulled me close so she could whisper in my ear, "It ain't a place. It's a woman we don't mention out loud. Megan Humphries is, well, she's a woman." Finally in disgust she let go of my arm. "You're a man. You know about those things."

I trailed them inside and we took up our places. Stout wouldn't dance the first one, and Erv had her arms folded over her chest like she was sulling. Even

Tate said no. So I got up and walked over to Darling Moore and took her away from three fish-eyed boys ready to ask her to dance.

I never looked back. I was going to have me a good time. Those three sisters could wait for some old tobacco-drooling man to come ask them to dance. I sure couldn't please them. But I could dance all night with this small bundle of blasting powder. She laughed easy at my way of talking. I guess I overdid the drawling part, which Darling liked the best. You kinda feed on that sort of attention and a feeling grows inside that you are as important as anyone there with the cutest little gal in the whole schoolhouse. I was doing that well.

"That Texan Jason still around?" I asked as we glided around.

"Oh, him. I haven't seen him since last week," she said. "Are you looking for him?"

"I got into a small discussion with him, was all."

"No, I remember you two had a fight. Did you resolve it?" she asked, her round, deep brown eyes all serious, looking up, questioning me.

"I hope so," I said, and moved off with her, making great circling waltz steps. Darling, I quickly figured, didn't realize Jason's true character, and she'd danced with him. Maybe it wasn't such a good idea letting Tate dance with him. Maybe she wouldn't see any more than Darling had. For the first time I doubted my theory that becoming familiar with his true character would help Tate get over Jason.

The fiddlers and the dulcimer players took a break,

and I took Darling back. Several boys her age seemed quick to intercede, and I excused myself since it wasn't fair for me to hog her all evening. I did see some regret in her eyes when we parted.

I was headed for the lemonade table. I swear Stout's boot toe flashed out, tripped and spilled me flat on my face. As I started to get up she was squatted beside me, and her firm hand was on my shoulder. She was holding me down—keeping me from rising up.

"H.B. Bentley," she whispered hard like, "that little doe-eyed Mormon gal will soon have you farming. One or the other of the Rice sisters have enough cattle that they own themselves to start that ranch you want. After this intermission you come back inside and dance with us." She paused. "I know how you hate damn dirt farming."

I swallowed hard, still unable to get up for her hand. "Yes, ma'am."

❖ 10 ❖

Reality is a tough pill to swallow, but Stout had given me a full dose of truth. With my back to the schoolhouse wall and sipping on the tin cup of sugary lemonade, I thought real strong on her warning. I appraised my situation; I hated farming worse than a chicken-killing dog. Stout was right—that dark-eyed Mormon angel surely would have me planting corn, bucking hay, and milking cows. I drew a deep breath, for her beauty still bothered me as I watched her standing in the doorway surrounded by several bucks her own age. A big waste, but ...

I went back inside after Darling and her admirers left the doorway. The notion of another cup of lemonade on my mind, I looked up to see three men crossing the room. I first figured they were coming for refreshments, and Stout even got a cup ready to serve them, but it was quickly obvious they wanted to talk to me.

"You must be H.B.," the older man said. "Gunther Craven. These are my boys, Ira and Seth."

I shook their hands and wondered how they knew me.

"Deputy Yarborough told us you shot one rustler and run off the rest."

"Blind luck was all," I said, almost embarrassed by Craven's words.

"Not hardly. Charlie Brackett says you'd do to ride with too. I just want to say we're proud to have your kind in this country. It looks like the North Cut's been hurt bad this year by this rustling, but with more folks like you getting to the bottom of it, we may get our country back from them varmints."

"Thanks," I said, and touched the brim of my hat to salute them. My conscience gnawed at me over how they were carrying on so about me doing so little. I was still feeling some embarrassed when Stout shoved Erv at me. Well, nearly at me. I realized the fiddles were crying for dancers to get out on the floor.

As I started to dance off I saw Darling across the room. There was a long look on her face like she halfway expected me to come back to her. It was over; this cowboy saw the error of his ways. Even if I never convinced the middle Rice sister I was seriously sparking her, I sure didn't need a hoe in my hand for the rest of my life. I turned my attention to dancing with the stiff-backed Erv.

"They're going to make you a real hero over that shooting business," Erv said.

I frowned at her. "You know the truth. There wasn't nothing to it. Let's drop the matter."

"I think it's getting to you." She kinda leaned back as we danced and inspected me for a moment. "It is getting to you, this business that these ranchers around here think you're a hero."

I swung her around, but I wanted to stuff the new clean kerchief around my neck in her mouth. Why did she have to needle me too? "I think we can talk about something else," I said close to her ear.

"Like what?"

"Like how we could take a break and go for a long walk."

She blinked her blue eyes in disbelief. *"What*ever for?"

"There's times courting you when it's damn hard," I said, and swung her around to the music. Her dress must have gone out too far and too high, for she reached with her right hand to quickly push it down.

"You did that to embarrass me," she accused. "And why are you courting me anyway?"

"Why not? You are old enough to be courted. I think you're very nice-looking." My temper was on a short fuse. This girl didn't know *anything!*

"You're blind," she said. "Besides, ten minutes ago you were dancing with that bug-eyed Darling Moore and didn't know I even exist."

"You're a hard person to convince. I have to take breaks from it."

"What about Darling?"

"She's too young," I said quickly.

She stopped dancing and looked at me as troubled as she could. "I'm her age."

I squeezed her hand hard and forced her to dance again before everyone in the schoolhouse knew our business. Damn, she was stubborn as my horse, Short. I never taught him much, and I sure wasn't winning Erv over.

"I'm her age," she whispered.

"You're more mature than she is, though," I said, having a hard time to even concentrate on the steps to the music.

"You're serious, aren't you?"

"Yes." But I turned, for trouble came through the doorway. They were drunk. Their familiar tall-crowned hats cocked back on their heads, Jason and Dobe stood rocking on their bootheels inside the doorframe. Dobe held a long double-barrel shotgun slung over his arm in a threatening manner.

"We come for you, H.B. Bentley," Jason said, and shaded his eyes with the side of his hand to see across the lighted room.

"There ain't no need for firearms inside," a tall gray-haired man said. "There's women and children in here."

Jason nodded, but neither he nor Dobe moved. They were staring hard at me. Jason held his gun hand out to make everyone stay. "We don't want the rest of you—just that damn H.B.!"

Erv moved in front of me defensively. Certainly I did not need her to shield me. I took her firmly by the shoulders and moved her aside.

When she was clear, I spoke. "I'll come outside. No need for any gunplay in here. Look, I'm not armed. Like the man said, there's children and womenfolk in here." Were they sober enough not do something foolish, like shoot up the schoolhouse? I hoped so.

Jason looked glassy-eyed. He wobbled on his bootheels like standing up was a big chore. I knew that many of the menfolk were ready to cave their heads in for scaring the womenfolk and kids. But I wanted the two outside, where fewer people would get hurt if something did happen.

"Want me to gutshoot him?" Dobe asked.

"No, I want him in a fair fight. Back outside," Jason said to his partner. When they stepped back I felt better for the safety of the innocent ones.

"Your gun's at the wagon," Stout said, her face ashen white under the deep tan.

"I don't need a damn gun."

"Yes you do!" Erv said, and grabbed my arm to stop me. "You can't go out there unarmed. Why, those two have pistols, and Dobe has that scattergun. Are you crazy, H.B. Bentley?" The dismay in her blue eyes hurt me.

"They won't shoot an unarmed man," I said, and moved her aside to head for the door.

"They might," Darling said in the throng of people around me. "H.B., don't go out there without a gun."

"That's a chance I'll take. We don't need shots fired around here. Everyone get back and let me handle them."

"The last time you tangled with them two, you needed me," Stout said.

"This time I'll fight harder. Thanks." I made her and the others stay back. I shook my head vehemently to stop several men ready to help. I headed directly for the door. Not that I was so brave, but I was bucking up to what was ahead for me and hoping no one else got hurt because of me.

"I'm coming out, boys," I shouted two steps from the door casing. "I'm not armed either!" My hands were held out away from my waist so it was obvious I had no gun on me.

Some cried, "Oh no!"

That didn't help my nerves, but I strode onto the porch and tried to adjust my eyes to the darkness. They were both mounted. Dobe still had the shotgun balanced on his lap.

"Next time, Bentley, I want you to be wearing that hogleg or you can die without it!" Jason said, and they reined their horses around to leave. As they charged their ponies off, Dobe let out a wild cry and fired both barrels in a flaming salute to the starry night.

For a long moment I let the tightness flow out of my muscles. Someone's arm slipped around my waist with a "Thank God." I was almost afraid to look, but when she straightened I saw it was Erv. She let go of me and stood up straight. Then Erv conspicuously shifted the waist of her dress to be proper as the others crowded outside around me.

"Thank goodness, he wasn't hit!" a woman cried out. I heard others say similar things as if the pair had shot at me, instead of at the sky. But how could they do any more than suspect the worst when they heard Dobe's scream and the shots?

"That's enough," Craven said. "We're running those two out on a rail. Get your horses, boys."

"Mr. Craven!" I called to them.

"What?"

"Let me handle those two; they're my problem."

"Not when they come here and endanger our families with their drunken antics."

"Let me try, sir?" I asked quietly. "They're pretty charged up on wildcat whiskey. I'll take care of them. This is my fight."

"They ever come back here and act like that, by God, I'll plant them in this school yard," Craven said, and went back inside the schoolhouse.

"What are you going to do about them?" Erv asked quietly.

I reached out and took her hand in mine. The music had restarted; others were going back inside. There was a lot of liberty in me taking Erv Rice's hand, with the hard palm and calluses at the base of each of her long, slender fingers, into mine. It was a still hand when I intertwined my fingers in hers and felt her respond ever so little to lock them. An encouraging sign, I figured.

"I'll track them down and have it out. Either we'll have an understanding after that or I'll settle it."

"H.B. Bentley, have you ever killed a man besides that rustler?"

"No, ma'am."

"Good."

"Why good?"

"I didn't want to believe you were some hardened killer, and me, well, you know."

"Holding hands with one?" I asked.

"Sort of. Let's talk about something else. What do you say to a girl like Darling Moore out here?"

She broke my train of thought. I was thinking about my meeting up with Jason and Dobe. What could I tell her?

"I never held hands out here in the school yard with Darling Moore or any girl."

"Ever?" She looked up in my face, then she had to touch her hair on the side like it was out of place.

"Why are you asking?"

"Because I can't decide whether you're some kind of a butterfly cowboy that rides around the country breaking girls' hearts or what."

"Butterfly cowboy? What the hell is that?" I frowned at her as we went hand-swinging along under the spray of stars.

"Oh, someone that roams around kissing girls like a damn butterfly goes from flower to flower."

"I'm not one of those." Why was I even in this conversation with Erv? I needed to go saddle my cow pony and trail those two drunks and have this out.

"A girl hates to be trifled with."

"Erv, I've never trifled with you!"

"You damn sure did! That day you rode up and kissed me, you trifled with me!"

I spun her around and kissed her. This time her lips

130

weren't smeared with that stinking Clover salve, and I kissed her like I meant it, with her bent over in my arms. I stood her up and felt her upper arms tremble under my hands.

"That's trifling," I said sharply.

Her arms loosely encircled my neck, and she looked up at me with her dreamy eyes. "You really did it that time." She held her mouth up and her eyes shut for me to kiss her again. I did. Then I crushed her against me, but I finally had to loosen my hold.

"Erv, I have to go find those two and settle this once and for all," I said, rocking her slender form in my arms.

"I think you should take us along."

"I think I better take you inside or I'll get too spoiled out here."

"You never told Darling that?"

"Dammit, Erv Rice, you—"

Her fingers closed my mouth, and I saw her wicked smile. I kissed her again and then took her back to the schoolhouse. I left her at the doorway and looked back once with regret at her silhouette standing against the light.

The dun snorted softly when I caught him. He'd probably been asleep, I decided, and led him back to the wagon. I heard soft voices coming across the school yard as I brushed off his back and prepared to put on the pads.

"We're going along," Stout said.

"I'd rather you let me handle it."

She shook her head. Tate was in the wagon and

handing out jeans for them to wear. "We're in this with you till the end."

"You just think you're running away," Erv said, putting her foot in one pants leg. "Look the other way, I'm dressing."

"Yes, she ain't yours yet," Tate teased, climbing out with their hats.

"Tate! I may never be either," Erv said.

"Don't talk so tough," Tate said. "Oh, dang, I forgot the guns."

"You don't need guns, these are just stupid drunk boys."

Erv wrestled up her jeans under her dress and shook her head in the starlight. "We know what we're doing. You can lead us, but we're taking guns."

"You ever shot a man?" I demanded.

"No, but you only have one notch more than we do," Erv said as she swung on my arm and then went to help Stout saddle up their horses. "Don't worry so, H.B., we can handle ourselves."

Outnumbered and outvoted, my all-woman posse and I were about to ride out. I was not that enthused. But there was not any need in complaining. The Rice sisters and I were going after them.

❖ 11 ❖

By dawn we were on the road to Flagstaff. There was no sign of the pair. They'd no doubt rode off in a drunken stupor into the timber somewhere, and we'd rode by them in the dark.

"We're close to Brackett's outfit. We can eat breakfast there and double back," Stout offered as we rested our horses and clung to our saddle horns. We were tired to the bone, and the thought of food appealed to everyone.

"Let's go. Catch a few hours shut-eye and we'll double back," I said, and noted their nods.

"What are we going to do about moving the cattle up?" Stout asked.

"Hainey wants to start in the morning so we can throw in with the others driving their herds to Flagstaff. Guess we'll quit our search at dark and go to the Quarter Circle Z. Some of us can get your wagon

133

back there and then start moving those cattle close to his schedule."

"Paw thinks more of our cattle will show up mixed in those other herds. We found a dozen head that belonged to ranchers on the east side of North Cut in our roundup," Stout said.

"You're missing more than a few head?"

"Yes, maybe a hundred head we counted on to sell," Erv said, joining us as we rode our weary horses toward Brackett's.

I tried to recall Hainey's remarks from his logbook about losses, but it seemed high too. What if those rustlers I ran into had taken that many head south to someplace to gain weight and wait for their branding to heal? Rice, Hainey, and Brackett only found a few steers with blotched brands around their camp. The cattle had to be somewhere. It would take at least a couple of months to hair up those brands so they looked natural.

"What's going on in your mind, H.B.?" Stout asked, looking at me hard.

"Those rustlers must have a place to keep those cattle south of the Breaks. You know of a place where there's grass and water south of here?"

Stout shook her head. "Rough country. It would be hard to find enough feed to hold any cattle. It's nearly all desert, and this late the feed would be short. You rode through it coming up here."

I agreed, but I hadn't come up the North Cut from the Salt. I'd rode over the mountain. "What's this river like south of here?"

"Goes in a narrow canyon for miles. Terrible tough country. They sure ain't got no cattle hid there," Stout said, looking to the other two for confirmation.

"They got them somewhere." I shook my head and listened to the black collie that came out to bark at us.

"Maybe H.B. will help us do Charlie's dishes," Tate said.

I swung around and frowned at her.

"Aw hell," Stout said, "him and Sonny are notorious poor housekeepers, and they always have more dirty dishes than five outfits. And we always wash them and tidy up when we stop off."

"You never said you'd help," Tate teased.

"You want my help, I'll help you," I agreed. The notion of tackling two weeks' dirty dishes held no appeal, as tired as I felt.

Brackett's outfit consisted of some low log buildings with board roofs topped with sod for insulation. The grass on the roofs was all brown and dead, and the sags in the ridgepole made them look like hills.

"What brings you all here?" Brackett said with a cup of coffee in his hand. "Light down. The dance must have been short."

"No, Jason and Dobe busted up the action looking for me, then left in a hurry."

"I thought they were fired," Brackett sputtered.

"They came looking for me was all," I said, dismounting heavy. "We need to beg a meal and a few hours' sleep. Charlie, you ever been all the way down the North Cut?"

He frowned as he waved the girls inside. "Naw, that's rough country, nothing but sheer canyons and hotter than hell. You gals can make something. I ain't that good of a cook."

I wish he'd seen the mean looks the Rice sisters gave him as they stood in the kitchen among the piles of dirty dishes and pans. But Brackett was still questioning me about the Lower North Cut. "Why you asking about that?"

"Those rustlers needed a place to heal those brands. I had never thought about it before. How many head they get of yours?"

"Fifty or so. I didn't have a good tally like Hainey did. Ain't much on bookkeeping. No, that country south is too rough, they couldn't go that way."

I didn't know—I'd never tried it. But I certainly wondered how those rustlers managed to do it. Tate brought me a cup of coffee. Brackett and I went out on the porch.

"It's farfetched that they could take that many steers and just disappear," Brackett said slowly.

"They're closer than we think, but I'm not familiar with this country." I looked across at the timber-clad mountains beyond. Brackett's place was at a higher altitude than Hainey's. The air was turpentine-smelling from the pines.

"I need to shut those two Texans down," I said, not looking at him. "Last night they came after me with a shotgun in that schoolhouse full of people. We lost them between here and the Pecan School House."

"Lots of country."

I agreed, realizing the futility of our ride, and went back inside to check on the meal's progress.

The girls had things under control. Erv was elbow-deep in suds. Tate was drying, and Stout tending the food on the stove. They waved off my offer to help them, to my relief.

"Those Texans will have sore heads and probably ride out of the country since they don't have jobs," I told them.

"Whatever you say," Erv said, looking at me for the answer.

"Kind of a wild-goose chase; sorry I drug you three along," I apologized.

"H.B., we'll stand by you. . . ." Erv looked up like she expected me to say more.

"I know that, but we have to be real about this business. Mr. Hainey and your paw want those cattle moved, and traipsing after those two ain't serving any good. We'll eat and go back after the wagon, then maybe by morning we can get the cattle going to join the drive." The weary Rice sisters agreed with a nod.

The late afternoon sun had the Quarter Circle Z drowning in purple and red colors when I rode in. The dog came barking to greet me. Hainey came out on the porch. A small puff of smoke from his cigarette drifted off where he stood against the porch post.

"Have a good time?" he asked in his warm, open way.

"Those Texas boys caused another ruckus, and we tried to find them last night. But they disappeared."

Hainey blew a thin stream of smoke out his nose. "They had to hurrah you one more time?"

"I guess."

"Rosita's got some leftovers she's saving for you. She's worried a hole in my bearskin rug fretting about you all day."

"I have not!" she denied vehemently.

"Well, he's all right," Hainey said, following me in. He sat astraddle a high-back chair and leaned over the back. He drew on the wadded-up cigarette and then blew the smoke out. "Guess you figured out, H.B., this will be a lean year for ranchers up here with all those cattle gone."

"I was kind of figuring I might get a job down around Hayden's Mill this winter." I knew he hated to tell me there wasn't enough money in his cattle deal to winter a cowboy on his payroll. I didn't aim to make it hard for him. Hainey was a good man, to my notion.

"I want you to make the drive to Flag with us."

"Good."

"We're going to be sure you get that reward too."

I busied myself eating the beans and cold bacon Rosita served. The reward would sure help. But I couldn't forget those rustlers. There had to be a place they took those cattle to heal them. I shook my head and drew a deep breath. The damn outlaws even denied me having a winter job.

"It'll be warm this winter down there," Hainey said.

"Yes, sir." Neither of us had much else to say. I still didn't put much stock in seeing any reward for the dead outlaw. I finished the meal, excused myself, and went to the bunkhouse. I fell on the bunk and slept hard.

Dawn came with Rosita's clanging triangle. A real cutting wind swept off the Mogollons. It woke me up sharply as I hurried to the shelter of the back porch and washed my face and hands. The water was cold, and the shock on my skin woke me more. I dried my face and hurried inside the cozy, warm, food-smelling kitchen.

"Better enjoy this. It'll be a week before we make Flag," Hainey warned.

"You reckon we could pack her and this kitchen along?" I asked.

"No." She shook her head. "I stay here and feed my chickens and milk my cow."

"We'll miss you," I said, sipping the burning hot coffee.

She put a plate of fried eggs and biscuits before me. "I think I'll keep you and send this old man away for the winter."

"Hey, hey, you can't do that," Hainey teased.

"Sometime I will try," she said, and passed his plate to him.

"There isn't a place they can take those steers that they rebranded and let them hair up, is there?" I asked Hainey. "Like down the North Cut?"

"No, that's too tough. Why?"

"They needed thirty to sixty days for the hair to

grow out on those steers they blotched over. Where did they rest them at?"

"Ain't much country south of here they could do that."

"Think on it; they've got maybe a hundred head of big two-year-old steers they can deliver to someone."

"I have, H.B. But damned if I can see how they'd get by a brand inspector. They sell them cattle and a brand inspector will be there. He'll see the blotched job."

I agreed, defeated. My answer wasn't coming, and I didn't know the country between there and the Salt River.

"There isn't a single valley they can hide in?"

"The only ones knew that route—if there is one—were the Apaches, and they slipped by the army a few times going and coming through there. Ain't a white man living could find it."

I accepted his answer and went back to eating. I slowly savored Rosita's cooking and dreaded the ride north. After breakfast at the bunkhouse I gathered my gear and put on my second shirt and the split-tail canvas duster that was a first-class wind shedder. My felt hat screwed down, I joined Hainey at the back door. We went and saddled in a cloud of dust swept off the yard. For my saddle stock, I took Short and the bay. Two horses would do for the drive. I saddled Short, and he jumped around some before I gained control. Mr. Hainey and me left heading into the gale.

Wind's a spoiler. It cheats you out of your vital senses and makes you work twice as hard for everything you accomplish. You turn your head down or away from it and don't see half the things you should. But keeping a horse going into the current is the hardest part when his natural inclination is to suck up his tail and turn his butt toward it.

The cattle were scattered, and we got there first. I swung south to bring them in. Hainey headed west to gather those back. The Rices arrived when I came in with a fair share. I smiled at Erv when she and Tate rode over. I didn't see Ewell.

"Where's your paw?" I asked.

"He'll be along," Erv said.

"Tell the man the damn truth," Tate said, looking at her older sister like she had hardly any patience left.

"You tell him," Erv said, and set spurs to her horse.

"When Paw gets upset he usually has him a long drink or two. You savvy?" Tate looked at me for help.

I nodded. A man sometimes couldn't face hard things in life. Their cattle business had turned bad, and Ewell Rice had counted on having a lot more to sell. I should have captured those men, not run roughshod over them and sent them packing before Hainey and the others arrived. Short got the blame for that. No time for regrets; we had cattle to gather. I booted the devil after more steers that needed rounding up.

The steers were lining out and headed for the road. Stout drove the wagon and waved to me. With her hat off and her hair blowing free, she looked almost pretty.

I fell in the drag without a word—someone needed to push the poky ones. Besides, the wind took the dust away so fast, it barely swept by at Short's knees. Mr. Hainey rode up in the lead, Tate on the right and Erv on the left. We were making a long string, and the cattle acted strangely docile. The wind became stronger, threatened to rip off my hat. I hoped that in the hills ahead we'd escape some of its force.

Stout had taken the wagon, the extra saddle stock tied to the tailgate, and gone ahead. She'd make evening camp somewhere ahead that Hainey had spoke of. I wondered about Brackett and Sonny, but dismissed it.

By midafternoon I saw Brackett and Pitts coming with more cattle. My heart quickened and I rode out to meet them. They drove in fifteen more head, and I noticed some had the Rice brand, and some Hainey's as well as Charlie's. The unexpected cattle drew a smile on everyone's faces as we drank metallic-tasting canteen water and gnawed on spicy, hard beef jerky.

"That's all we found," Charlie said.

Everyone nodded.

"It'll sure help. Maybe those guys in the east found some more of our stock," Hainey said to cheer us up. The junipers were helping break some of the wind, but as soon as we mounted up, the wind would find us.

"You all right picking up drag?" Erv asked.

"Fine," I said, and exchanged a private smile.

I swear she blushed. She quickly turned and mounted her horse. I hated to tell her I was leaving the country after Flagstaff. She would for sure think I was a butterfly cowboy. I stuck my toe in the stirrup, thinking how I'd tell her, when Short broke in two. He went to grunting like an old hawg as he bucked, trying to rub me off every jump in a juniper bough or piñon on the hillside.

That good-for-nothing worthless pile of glue and soap—I'd sell him cheap in Flag and buy a damn mule to ride. If Short read my mind about my intentions, it made not a difference to him, he only bucked higher and wilder. I was pulling on the bits for all I was worth. Short was having a tantrum that wouldn't quit, and I was considering getting off and shooting him. Except if I got off, my gun was in my saddlebags, and I couldn't shoot him while I was in the saddle. The air was blue with my profanity. I called that goose-livered rotten crowbait of an excuse for a horse every-thing I'd ever heard, learned, or knowed. Then he finally did it, loosened me from the saddle, and next thing I knew, I was airborne. I turned over twice and landed on my pride harder than I intended.

Erv came running in her boots at a pigeon-toed gait, her knees nearly locked together. I almost laughed at her stride, but I hurt too bad. My pride was worse off than any other part. She was on her knees, in my face.

"Are you all right?" she asked, her gloved hand touching my cheek.

"Fine," I said, nodding my head slightly with her face only inches from mine.

"I thought every bone in your body would be broken."

There she was kneeling right before me. "I'm fine," I said. "I think the others are coming."

"Oh, yes," she said, and wet her lips before she sat back on her legs.

"Help me up," I said as she drew herself up.

"You sure you're all right?" She steadied me and then looked me up and down.

"Fine," I said, seeing Tate bringing old Short back.

"Good, I'll ride him," Erv said, and took the reins. "You take my gray."

Before I could shout "No!" she put her foot in the stirrup and swung in the saddle, with me barely peeking. Short would explode. I knew he would. Erv put her spurs to him, and the cussed cow pony galloped away like a dead broke horse. That traitorous son of a b.

❖ 12 ❖

More outfits joined up with their herds that afternoon. All day there were introductions and reintroductions at the campgrounds where we'd halted. I knew lots of them from the dances.

Mr. Hainey and I were eating some of Stout's brown beans and sourdough biscuits, sitting on our haunches and enjoying the heat from the fire on our faces. The fire's warmth drove a lot of the wintry chill away.

"I don't think we gained a dozen head," Hainey offered.

"Guess those rascals got away with the rest."

"They got several, but we may have bigger troubles. I heard a big outfit's bringing their cattle in. One of the Craven boys said the Double T has maybe a thousand head they're taking to market. That'll hurt the price too."

"Who are they?"

"Double T's an English outfit bought out a bunch of ranches."

"Reckon they need a cowboy?" I asked.

"They might. I don't think you'd like working for them. They're a haughty bunch. But one thing, rustlers would be afraid to mess with them larger ranches like that. They hire their own regulators. These are good beans, Stout." He waved his fork at her and nodded his appreciation.

"Might ought to burn them, then I'd get out of cooking," she said, and exchanged a warm smile with us.

I excused myself and went to relieve some of the others on herding duty so they could eat. Herd duty was pretty slow work. The cattle grazed some, and the ranchers hoped to hold the weight on them during the drive.

"Going all right?" I asked Erv, riding up beside her.

"Fine, they've all settled in pretty well for a mixed bunch."

"I've got to tell you something." I wasn't too certain how to say it.

She blinked her blue eyes at me. "Yes?"

"I'm not going to have a job with Hainey after we deliver these cattle. That means I'll have to go back to Salt River country and work on some farm for a while, I guess."

"Maybe something will work out," she said, looking troubled.

"Ain't what I want either."

She nodded and rode off. I felt better. She wasn't

hopping mad, and I hadn't lost her. Maybe I could figure out a way. Damn, a man can feel like a king one minute, and the next like a mangy cur with his tail between his legs sneaking up an alley.

I began to take a turn around the cattle who were scattered out in the meadow, picking grass and looking up every once in a while like they'd take a chance and bust off for the pine-clad hills. If any of those steers or cull cows knew they were headed for the butcher shop, they'd probably try to do just that.

Sundown came early in October, and we had the cattle bedded. Most were chewing their cuds with their old bellies full of rich cured grass. There were still some fights over who was boss. They were mostly yearlings, and that meant they were prone to spook at anything.

"You sing or play a mouth harp?" Craven asked.

"Don't do neither very good," I admitted.

"Then just talk to them as you ride around, so you won't spook them if you accidentally ride into or over a sleeping one. I've seen these kind of cattle act quiet as milk cows and then, at the drop of a hat, stampede at nothing."

"Yes, sir," I said, and touched my hat politely since he was the other co-boss with Mr. Hainey for the drive.

"I never heard. Did you find them Texans the other night?"

"No, sir, they took a powder after the deal they pulled at the dance."

"They need to be run out of the country," Craven said grimly, and rode his horse off in the twilight. There were four of us herders, and relief was due at midnight. I rode the dun, and he was head-down-serious, walking around the dark blotches of sleeping, grunting bovines. Once or twice an individual animal off in the dark herd would bawl several times and then go quiet.

I whistled awhile and then, figuring the girls were in camp, I sang another verse about Ol' Blue, the lead steer.

> Old Blue knew Miss Sue,
> Who lived on the slough.
> He took those cowboys there.
> She fed Ol' Blue corn,
> And she tooted their horn,
> And danced naked for them on a dare.
> Hi la, hi lo . . .

The wind had quieted down, but the night air was crisp with a promise of an early frost. Erv rode out with some hot coffee in a jar for me.

"I really was upset about you talking of leaving," she said as we rode side by side. I sipped on the still hot liquid.

"Yes." I stopped my horse and held my hand out to stop her as I studied the outline of two riders coming around the herd. They weren't the other herders; I knew those riders' silhouettes and the shape of their hats against the night sky.

"Howdy," I said, leaning back and slowly reaching in my saddlebags for the Colt.

"Who are they?" Erv whispered.

"We've come to settle this once and for all," Jason said.

"It ain't the time or the place," I said quickly. "These cattle aren't trail-broke. You cause them to run, someone will get hurt."

"Ain't no worry to me. Is it to you, Dobe?"

Dobe drove his horse in beside Jason and spit tobacco off to the side. "The sum-a-bitch Kenyon that fired us has his cattle here, ain't he?" He spit again. "Don't matter to me if they all died."

I could barely make them out in the starlight. The Colt's hard rubber grips were tight in my right hand. Did I dare do anything with Erv there, and the herd sure to spook at any commotion?

"You guys are fools!" Erv hissed. "You stampede these cattle, the cattlemen will hang the two of you, and I'll help them."

"Tough talk, sister," Jason said.

"You two better get out of here," I ordered, and cocked the Colt. The click was unmistakable, and both Jason and Dobe sat up in their saddles. "I'm not counting past ten, and if you two aren't gone, then you better have your dues paid for that place up there." I used my spur to make the dun horse sidestep so I wasn't so close to Erv if they decided to shoot it out.

"So you're finally armed," Jason said.

He was going for his gun. I knew he was. Even in

the dark I could see his intentions. Was he suicidal? Didn't he think I'd shoot him?

"H.B.!" Erv screamed a warning. Sam Colt bucked in my hand. The night belched orange gunfire, followed by the sharp report of two pistols. Jason pitched off his horse, and Dobe responded by spurring his horse west. The cattle were on their feet. I knew there would be no containing them. One minute they were quiet, the next they were a bawling rage of thundering hooves. The massive wave swept down the valley westward in a great flood.

"Undo your slicker," I shouted at Erv. "Use it to wave at them. We need to circle them to the right."

"I'm coming," she said, trying to pull the strings free. I jammed the Colt in my waistband and spurred the dun toward the front of the herd, screaming at the cattle to turn them sideways as I rode to the point to find the leaders.

I saw Dobe riding ahead of the leaders in the silver light, whipping his horse down the valley. The racing cattle were about to overtake him on both sides. Despite his frantic lashing of his horse, I saw he was in the center of the herd at the front of the stampede. I had no time to worry about him, but Dobe's position was serious.

My cow pony ran all out. He was fast catching the point cattle, and I pressed him harder into the inky night. One misstep or stumble in the darkness and we'd be down under the sea of lunging cattle. Using my slicker for a flag, I tried to spook them to the side. For a fraction of a minute or longer the dun and I were in a very vulnerable place. If the point animals didn't turn, we were directly in the herd's path. Sometimes you had to shoot the lead animals to turn them. My voice rasped in a continuous scream. For a split second I considered shooting them. I fired the Colt twice in the air, and to my relief the leaders finally swung aside.

The surge of cattle began to slow in a circle. They gradually piled up, and that broke their stride. I saw Erv waving her oilskin and drew a deep breath realizing she was safe. I wondered about Dobe. There was no sign of him. The notion made me sick.

"Who fired those first shots?" Craven asked, reining in his heaving horse.

"It was do or die for Erv and I. Jason came back for more."

"He rode in looking for trouble," Erv said.

"Where's he at?" Craven asked, twisting around in his saddle.

"Back there where it started. I shot him. And Dobe was trying to outrun the cattle when the stampede started. I haven't seen him since then." The grim thought of someone run over by hundreds of sharp hooves was not nice.

"That's his stupid fault. Could be worse," Craven said. "You and Erv did a great job of turning them, H.B."

"Thanks," I said, and drew a deep breath. Too close for comfort. Those stupid Texas boys were nothing but a big problem to me. Maybe it was over. I wondered if Dobie had survived.

Erv and I worked around the cattle and were joined by the other night wranglers. The herd acted calm again, except for a few steers bawling like they'd lost their best friend. Without much to say to each other, the four of us went back to slowly circling the cattle. The two other wranglers spoke briefly when we rode up together after another round.

"Sure thought they were gone to the Grand Canyon," the one called Skipper said.

"Say yeah and my wages with them," his pard said with a laugh.

Filled with relief, we visited a few moments, then went back to the herd. Erv was quiet, and I sang about Ol' Blue. Sonny and Brackett came out for the second shift to relieve us.

"Your problems are over, H.B., Jason's dead. They also found Dobe's body out there," Brackett said, and rode on by with a nod to Erv.

I'd figured as much. One more thing to ruin this drive for me. I sure wished they'd quit the country and left me alone.

"I know you're taking this hard," Erv said when we rode back to the wagon.

"My fault. I brought my problems to the drive."

"No, your problems are ours."

I dismounted heavily and began to undo the cinch. "I appreciate that."

"Damn, that Texan begged you to shoot him, huh?" one of the Craven brothers asked as the two crowded in. "Never seen the likes. Why, you had them cattle in hand quicker than I ever believed was possible. Dark as hell, night and all that."

A hand clapped my shoulder, and someone passed me a flat bottle of whiskey. I took a small jolt to be friendly, handed it back, and thanked them. There was no way to separate fact and fiction. I knew the whole thing would stand despite my denials. I wanted to talk to Erv privately, but she took my horse away and left me with them.

"His pard got trampled, huh?" one of the cowboys asked.

"Yes. He tried to outrun them." I saw Hainey coming in the firelight.

"Lucky one of our bunch didn't get hurt," he said. "Boy, they were crazy to even try that."

"They figured they had nothing to lose by stampeding the herd," I said. "Guess the bad blood between us ate 'em up."

Hainey agreed with a nod. "We need to talk."

The Craven boys excused themselves, and we stepped aside into the shadows beside the Rices' wagon.

"If this big outfit gets to Flagstaff first, there won't be a railcar left to ship our cattle on," Hainey said. "That means we'll have to hold ours out on grass or take a lower price."

"What can we do?" I asked.

"We need to move respectably so we beat them there."

"No problem," I said. "What can *I* do?"

"I want to push them closer to Flagstaff. They say

153

there is grass at Mormon Lake. We'll have to make a
dry camp tomorrow night. That means a long push to
Mormon Lake the next day. But I've got a special job
for you."

"What's that?"

"It could be dangerous, but I think you can handle
yourself. We need you to scout the Double T herd
and get a notion how fast they're coming and get back
with word. You leave before daybreak and meet us
day after next at Mormon Lake. If we have to hustle
from there to beat the Double T, it's fairly flat into
the railhead from the lake. If we got time, we can rest
them around the lake for whatever days we have and
regain some of the weight loss."

"What about Jason and Dobe?"

"We'll bury them first light. Don't worry, there was
nothing else you could have done. They drew their
own troubles."

I wished I felt like Hainey did. A heavy knot of guilt
fitted around my neck like a heavy collar. I wanted to
shake the picture of my Colt belching death in a long
orange flame. The acrid smell of spent powder was
still in my nostrils. The outline in the starlight of Dobe
racing ahead of the dark flood of cattle stayed in my
head.

I waded over and poured myself a cup of coffee.
Hunkered down, I studied the glowing red logs and
sipped the hot liquid. The whiskey was burning a hole
in my stomach. Strange how a small amount of liquor
usually made me feel easy, but this time it worked the
opposite.

I hardly slept. Three or four times I awoke and jerked straight up in my bedroll to a sitting position, almost trembling with fear. At dawn I saddled Baldy at Erv's insistence that I take the best horse in the outfit.

"You be careful out there," she said, restraightening the saddle pad I'd just placed on the horse's back.

I swung the saddle up, and she moved me aside like I was too dumb to cinch up my own horse. I stood back, almost perturbed at her busybody ways.

"I don't want you taking any chances. Hear me? Those big outfits like the Double T play for keeps." She struggled to cinch the front girth.

"Erv," I said, and used my arm to move her aside to finish. "I know how to handle myself. I'm not going to start a war with them. All I'm going to do is see how they're coming."

"They won't know that, and they might shoot first and ask questions later."

I kissed her on the side of the face and stepped up in the saddle. Her hand flew up to cover the spot on her cheek like I had burned her.

"Listen, butterfly cowboy, you better meet us at Mormon Lake tomorrow night or I'll ..."

I reined up Baldy. "You'll what?"

"Come looking for you!" Erv slapped Baldy on the rump and I left camp.

✦ 13 ✦

I could see the Double T herd coming a long time before I heard their constant bawling. The pines on the hills were almost obscured by the dust in the air. By my estimation there was over a thousand head, and that took up lots of railroad cars.

I had seen their chuck string and swung north to catch them. There were two wagons in tandem with the chuck; one hauled their bedding. There was a large remuda of solid-colored horses, for even at a distance a man can see the color of a horse herd. The Double T had few white markings in their string. What had Mr. Hainey said? They were a haughty bunch. Well, I poked Baldy in the sides and headed for where the cook was fixing to set open his tailgate.

"Howdy," the cook said, looking up at me, blinking his eyes like he never expected company. "My name's Nolan."

156

"Nice to make your acquaintance. H.B. here. I was thinking I might buy some groceries."

"Light your bones, boy. Mr. Temple ain't much on feeding strays, but he ain't the cook for this outfit."

"He own this whole thing?" I asked, looking back toward the dust of the herd, still several miles south.

"No, some English lord named Canterberry owns it. Mr. Temple is the main boss for him."

I took up an ax from the side of the wagon and went to busting kindling out of wood he had in the belly pan. The best way to a cook's heart was to help him. While most cowboys stood back and acted like it was below their dignity, I liked to eat.

"You looking for work?"

"Nope, just drifting. You all must be hurrying to get to the railhead." I quit chopping and turned my ear so I could hear his answer.

"Naw, we're going to rest a few days on some grass Mr. Temple has spotted to fill out the cattle. Been dry this fall where we are."

I was relieved and ready to ride back. Mr. Hainey could take his old sweet time if that was true. But I decided it would look too suspicious if I didn't linger around and eat some of Nolan's cooking.

He started some coffee water over the fire and gave me some raisin-cinnamon biscuits left over from breakfast. They were a little dry but sure were good. I busted some more wood, and he busied himself whipping up fresh biscuits for the evening meal. The camp helper, a young boy with a bad case of eruptions on his face, peeled potatoes.

"You a cowboy?" he asked me as I sipped the first fresh cup of Nolan's coffee.

"Sometimes," I said, seeing some of the drovers headed in. I rose to my feet to get ready to meet them.

"I'm going to be a cowhand one of these days," the youth said, and pitched another potato in the pot. "Then someone else can do this damn women's work."

"Good luck to you," I said, and stepped over by the cook.

"They'll be mad," Nolan said to me. "I missed getting a deer with my rifle this morning. All they'll have for supper is fatback again. Mr. Temple wants to make a good showing to the Englishman on this sale. He won't allow us to kill a beef."

I studied on that notion of not allowing the cook to even kill a single steer for camp meat. Strange orders for a big outfit—who'd miss one? Or was Temple afraid someone like Nolan might discover a blotched brand?

Part of the hands rode in, dismounted, and waded over in their bull-hide batwing Texas chaps. Some nodded at me; others just looked bland and poured themselves coffee with a grunt.

"My name's Tom," one offered, and stuck out his hand.

"Boys, this is H.B. He's headed through and needed a meal," Nolan announced.

"Nice to meet you, Tom," I said, and shook his hand.

Others less friendly mumbled off their names and sat down on the ground with their coffee cups as if considering me.

"You working?" one asked. He was sprawled on his side on the ground, considering his cup.

"Right now I'm looking," I said.

"I figure this outfit will lay half of us off in Flag," the cowboy said, and then blew on his coffee. That drew a grumble from the rest. They reminded me of a lot of old sore-back horses. Lot more fun to cowboy with the Rice sisters than this crew.

I noticed one puncher kept staring at me when he thought my back was turned. I didn't know him, but something was bothering him more than who I was. Didn't make sense. I'd never worked with him or I'd sure remember his face.

"Guess jobs are scarce all over," I said, thanked them, and mounted Baldy. As I rode away I felt that cowboy burning a hole in my back. Why?

I took a shortcut as it was getting late. I figured the pine-covered hills would be easy enough to cat-hop Baldy over rather than ride around them. The daylight was growing short, but I hoped for a little moonlight. If I couldn't make a connection with Hainey and the others, I hoped to be with them by sunup and slow him up. No need in pressing for Flag if they didn't need to.

Baldy was picking his way up the mountainside on a game trail. I looked back across the shadowy grasslands that spanned for miles to the far horizon. I saw a couple of specks and studied them hard. Two riders were trailing me. I halted Baldy, wondering why and who.

Then I turned my horse's head west and we scrambled up the hillside. The notion someone was on my back trail was unsettling. No one hardly took exactly the same path when they were cutting across country. Besides, I wasn't headed for anywhere in particular, like a town or ranch, just the trail herd.

Baldy carried me over the divide and started down through the dark timber. The sun was gone and twilight lighted the way, but in the trees there was darkness. We passed through the stripes of the ponderosa trunks. I paused and listened for my pursuers, hearing nothing but a coyote's mournful yips. There was no sound of either horse or man on the hill above me. I pushed Baldy on.

The night air quickly grew cold. Baldy's breath even turned to steam as we found the base of the hill and rode north along the edge of the timber for cover instead of out in the silvery open grassland. Maybe I had seen things. Why would anyone want to trail me?

One way to find out was to build a fire. If they were looking for me, a fire would sure bait them. I found a large dead tree fall, one dry and brittle enough to break off the branches and make a roaring fire. I tied Baldy in the trees and left him saddled. Then I spread my bedroll out and began to make camp. The fire's flames soon licked the sky, and anyone within miles could see it. I stuffed the bedroll with pine boughs till it looked like a man inside. Satisfied the fire would be enough of a beacon, I took my Colt and the cartridges from the saddlebags and climbed on top of a large house-sized boulder to wait. The trap was set.

I listened to hoot owls and a hundred night critters. Sprawled on my belly, I deeply wished that I had the bedroll for warmth even though the sun had heated the rock all day.

They came out of nowhere; only the clatter of hooves announced their arrival. The night became afire with pistol shots, and before I could even find a target to shoot, they were gone, whipping their horses away in the inky night.

"We got that son of a ..." The rest of his cussing faded in the night and pounding hooves.

"Yeah, we can tell ..." I couldn't hear who they'd tell, for they were wasting no time in fleeing their ambush. I hurried down to put out the fires in my bedroll. The shots had several spots smoking that would have been in me. Damn the luck. I still wasn't certain who they were or why they wanted me out of the way. They weren't worried about me knowing their plans to hold off the cattle and to let 'em regain some weight. No, it took a stronger reason than my knowledge of that to bushwhack me.

Mormon Lake looked serene. Baldy came along at a fast jog. The pony had a single-foot gait that was smooth as silk, and I'd kill to own him. The green wagon was resting near the shore, so I knew I'd beat the cattle. I saw Erv come around and smile at me.

"You look plumb tuckered out," Erv said, wiping her hands on the apron and watching me unsaddle.

"I am. It's been a long ride. But that big outfit ain't going to beat us to Flagstaff."

"That's good news. Mr. Hainey and the others were certainly upset wondering."

I put my arm around Erv's shoulder and herded her toward the coffeepot. I was ready for some form of refreshment. My sum total of food for the day had been some rock-hard jerky. I needed to replenish my saddlebags too.

"You're getting plumb familiar for a man fixing to leave this country," she said as I poured a cup.

"Can't help that," I said.

"There's a small place for sale up on Whitman Creek. Aw, you probably ain't ready to be tied down with no two-bit place."

"Would you show me?" I asked.

"Stout could, I guess." She shrugged her shoulders.

"Why not you?"

"I've never felt real good since all this happened." She shook her head. I heard her breathe with a deep exhalation. "I don't know how to tell you, but Stout has some claim on you first."

"I've never courted Stout!"

Erv shook her head and went off to the food making. "I can't do that to her."

"Do what to her?" I demanded.

"You know! Take you away from her!" she said, and slammed a big kettle on the tailgate for finality.

I shook my pounding head and sipped the strong coffee. My God, what did I have to do? I searched across the wide grassland to the east and wondered if the Double T bunch had counted me dead. Maybe a bath in the lake would help revive me. I borrowed a towel and headed out on foot to find a secluded cove. There was no way for me to ever win that girl's favor, no way.

❖ 14 ❖

"**Y**ou know a man can catch cold taking a durn bath?" Hainey asked as I dried my hair, grateful for the high sun.

"I'll take a chance once in a while." I sat down on a driftwood log on the shoreline to put on my socks and boots.

"Erv says you had some good news?" Hainey asked, dismounting.

"Word in the camp is they're going to graze the herd someplace before they push in. Said the season was real dry where they were coming from, and they wanted more weight on the cattle."

Hainey nodded. "That's good news."

"Except someone didn't want me alive to tell that."

"Huh?"

"They filled my bedroll full of lead last night. I saw them trailing me after I left their camp."

"Regulators?" Hainey frowned at me.

"No, some cowboys. A regulator would have been certain I was dead. Those two rode off like it was all over after putting several slugs in the bedroll."

"You see them?"

"Not good enough to identify them. It was dark."

"Why did they want you dead?" Hainey asked. "They didn't know your purpose for being there."

"It wasn't that. I been figuring they wanted me out of the way for a better reason than spying on their movement, if they even knew that was my purpose for being there. I never got a clear look at the one rustler held me up before Short kicked him. More I think on it, he could have been at the Double T camp yesterday. This one drover kept staring at me the whole time I was in their camp like something was wrong." I tried hard as I could to remember something about the rustler that stopped me.

"Huh? You ain't making good sense."

"Mr. Hainey, a cowboy rode in the Double T's camp yesterday, and he kept staring at me. I couldn't place him, but there was something familiar about him. I'm thinking he had a real fine, long hand-twisted mustache like the rustler that had the drop on me."

"Lots of pokes got that," Hainey said.

"Lots of cowboys don't keep staring at your back like they're trying to pin something on you when you ain't looking."

"Why would a rustler be working for the Double T outfit?" Hainey asked. "That don't make good sense. That Lord Whoever don't need money from his ranch.

He's probably got money enough over there in England to burn wet mules with dollar bills for heat on a rainy day."

I agreed and finished pulling on my boots. "Well, what next?"

"Why don't you and the Rice girls go into Flagstaff. You can check with the law on that reward. I know they want to get some things. We'll bring the cattle in Friday, and you make sure and have some pens reserved for us."

"That's your job," I said, feeling he was letting me off light.

"You've done enough work for this outfit already. Plan on doing that in the morning."

"I will, sir. I'll take care of that. Oh, Mr. Hainey?" I called out to him as he mounted up and started to ride off.

"What?"

"Do you know much about women?"

A warm grin spread over his leathery face and he slapped his saddle horn. "Not very much. I've been trying to figure out Rosita for a passel of years."

"I got me a wildcat by the tail in this deal. I'm partial to Erv, and she thinks I ought to be with Stout."

"What's Stout think?"

"She's a good friend, but I never asked her."

"She's a mighty levelheaded gal. I'd just ask Stout to release you. She's got more sense than most grownups. But those girls are like the daughters I never had. I sure couldn't take no sides." Mr. Hainey reined his horse around and grinned again. "Guess I didn't help you much."

"Thanks anyway, I'll have to work it out." I let him go. But I was still perplexed how to handle Erv and her hidebound loyalty to Stout. All I knew for certain was I was damn sure wearing my Colt into Flagstaff.

Morning came with a blanket of clouds. They could be front-runners for some Gulf of California moisture. The girls hustled around getting on their best dresses to wear to town. I took my war bag from the wagon. They put their jeans on underneath, and I almost laughed. If they'd owned little box hats with veils and flowers, I swear they'd have worn them instead of their cowboy hats, which looked a damn sight better to me.

Midday we saw the smoke of a Santa Fe locomotive billowing up in the sky. I had Mr. Hainey's gray, Erv rode Short—who acted like a well-mannered cow pony—Stout had a big dun, and Tate rode a bright paint pony.

"H.B., you figure we'll be there by dark?" Tate asked.

"Should be. Mr. Hainey figures it's twenty-five miles or so; takes two days of easy moving to drive the cattle there, he says."

"I'm having me some ice cream at the drugstore," Stout announced.

"That sounds better than peaches," I said aloud. Erv wasn't saying much. She'd sullied up again, and I wasn't sure how to patch things up. I liked Stout, but

I sure didn't crave to court her. And because Stout saw me first was no reason she had the rights to me. Lord, I couldn't make good sense out of the whole thing. I aimed to have some fun in Flagstaff. Maybe get good and drunk. I still had my wages from Mr. Daniel. Maybe I needed to throw a ringtail rooster of a drover party where you drank bad whiskey, hugged and loved on some shady ladies, and barked at the moon till your money was gone.

"You going to the law's first?" Stout asked while riding beside me.

"I ain't sure," I said. If that reward fell through, I would be disappointed. It was a matter of being afraid the answer was no. What then?

Our horses boogered when the train engine gave a sharp hoot. We were at the Santa Fe tracks, staring at all the stores and saloons on Front Street. The last of the sun shone on snowcapped Mount Humphrey above us. The temperature had begun to drop, and we headed for Dunlap's wagon yard. We stabled the horses and walked the last two blocks to the Cattlemen's Hotel, a two-story affair with a balcony around the second floor.

I opened the door to the hotel lobby. Two cowboys stopped, and I read the surprise on their faces.

"That's him!" one shouted. They were grasping for leather. I knew we wanted out of that situation.

I whirled and shoved Stout outside, then jerked the door closed. My bootheel caught and I fell on my butt as the frosted glass above me busted into great shards from the blasts of their guns. Inside, women were screaming at the top of their lungs.

Huddled down beside the door, I drew my Colt and looked around to check on the Rice sisters. They looked pale but safely seated on the porch floor.

"Stay here," I said, and gun first, I burst into the lobby. I saw the fleeing heels of the pair going down the hall for the back door.

"You girls get the law. That's those rustlers!" I shouted, and took pursuit.

I rushed past several ashen-faced ladies and shocked customers in the hotel's lobby with my gun in hand. The tile floor was slick under my leather boot soles as I raced to catch up with the pair. They were the same two from the cabin; I recognized the baldheaded one even though he was wearing his hat.

The dark alley was empty when I burst into it. I ran to the next street, but there was no sign of them as I stood with the Colt in my hand. They were gone. What should I do next? Find the law—they'd arrest this pair. I started back as Tate and Erv caught up.

"Stout went for the marshal," Erv said, looking me over inspectively like I might have a bullet hole in me that I missed. "You all right?"

"I'm fine, but it was too close a call. I never expected to find them here." I shook my head, still confused about the entire setup.

"Are we going to the marshal's office?" Erv asked.

"After we learn those birds' names from the desk clerk." I stuck the Colt in my waistband. I figured to have some rest and relaxation in Flag, not more trouble.

"Mr. Bentley?" the clerk began, looking over his glasses at me.

"Yes, sir. What were their names?" I asked.

"The two gentlemen who, ah, shot at you?"

"Exactly. What are their names?"

"Mr. Smith and Mr. Jones, according to their signatures, and they hail from Fort Worth." He pointed to the ledger, then he turned it around for me to read.

Erv looked hard at me. "That isn't their names, is it?"

"It is in Flagstaff," I said. "Give me the key to their room."

"Oh, that would not be possible," the clerk said.

"Give me the key," I said, holding my hand out for it.

"I can't do that."

"You can or you'll face the wrath of about twenty cattlemen coming in here." I held out my hand expecting the key.

"We're going to look in their room?" Tate asked.

"Yes, we're going to learn their real names before the law gets here," I said, and closed my hands on the pass key. "Which room?"

"Two-twelve." The clerk shook his head in disapproval as we headed up the stairs. I wasn't sure of anything, and when I stuck the key in the lock I did so from the side, making the girls stand back.

The door opened and I moved in with my Colt in hand.

"You girls look around the beds." I stuck the gun back in my waistband and went to looking in their saddlebags. There were bills of sale for horses. It was an old trick—horse thieves usually carried them in case they are stopped with a stolen animal. Then I found a letter in a woman's handwriting to a Curly Stephens.

"Curly," I read aloud,

> I hope this letter finds you in good health. I want to quit Madame Flourie and join you in Arizona. There must be a parlor house needs me there. Write and let me know. I sure miss you and know you're doing good in the livestock business. Love, Misty Rose.

"Who's Curly Stephens?" Tate asked.

"Oh, Tate, that woman was a shady lady wrote that letter," Erv said. "Who cares who Curly was?"

"He's also one of those two rustlers that shot at me," I said.

"What rustlers?" the big man with the badge on his tweed vest asked from the doorway.

"The ones that shot out the glass downstairs. And have tried to kill me several times of late. You must be the law." I put out my hand to shake his.

"I am, sir. Marshal John McAllen. You must be the H.B. Bentley who the lady spoke of. Where did this pair of shooters go?"

"I'm not sure, Marshal. They probably have taken their horses and rode out for parts unknown."

He shook his head. "No, they didn't get any horses. I sent two of the town's watchmen to warn everyone not to let two men dressed like Texas cowboys have any horses tonight without my approval."

In our search we found a bill of sale for a bay horse and a bank deposit book from Fort Worth with the name Henry Miles as the depositor. The funds were zeroed out almost a year before.

Rustlers lodged in a cattlemen's hotel? The whole matter was confusing. Obviously these outlaws were in touch with lots of money or expected some. But they couldn't have been the ones shot up my bedroll, because they were checked into the hotel while I was being shot at.

"H.B., you've got something on your mind?" Stout asked.

"I wish I knew more than I do. What if those guys were waiting? Marshal, I need to talk to some cattle buyers about them."

"We'll have to wait till morning. It's late, they'd all be at home. I'd like to go along, though, when you do that. Come by my office in the morning, we'll go talk to them. Maybe one of them can shed some light on this pair. You will excuse me, I have rounds to make."

"Yes, sir, we haven't eaten either." My hungry belly reminded me how long it had been since my last meal. "Reckon we'll go find supper."

"Certainly. You all are safe here in Flagstaff. This shooting is highly unusual outside of the saloons and bars. The young lady says you're the man we heard so much about lately. The one gunned down Buster Kimes?"

"That's me." I didn't want to elaborate too much—I only wanted my reward. If McAllen knew about it, maybe there actually was a reward.

"So I'll see you in my office in the morning, Mr. Bentley. Ladies, good evening. I'm sure my deputies will have this pair in custody by then. Sorry your first night in Flagstaff was so rough. We usually have a better handle on things."

The lawman left. We closed up the room and went downstairs to the hotel lobby.

"H.B., can we change clothes?" Tate asked at the foot of the stairs. "I promise we'll hurry."

I agreed, and they registered for one room for the three of them and rushed upstairs, their bootheels clicking on the iron. I sat down in a leather chair and read the Denver paper.

I listened to the desk clerk's dozen explanations to new patrons about the broken frosted glass and who was responsible. Behind the paper I smiled as the clerk detailed how the first criminals in the history of the hotel drew blazing guns and how, amazingly, the man they wanted dead had gone unscathed.

The girls, without their jeans under their skirts, hatless, with shawls on their shoulders and faces scrubbed clean, came down the stairs. I rose to meet them.

"We could go get some sardines and crackers to eat in our room," Erv said as we stood outside the salon.

"We're supposed to be having a good time," I whis-

pered in her ear. "Try hard to have some." Tate
nearly giggled, and Stout nodded with approval.

The waiter showed us to a table with a linen table-
cloth like a woman's skirt that hung to the floor. There
was polished silverware and china plates for us to use.

"What in the hell do they feed folks on these fancy
platters?" Erv asked, indicating the dishes.

"Beef, potatoes . . . They may have fish even."

"You order us something we'd eat," Stout said,
looking around like she had second thoughts about
the restaurant. I took care of the ordering.

They brought French onion soup for the first course.
It looked dark brown, like a mudhole in a cow lot.
The girls gave it two or three quick skeptical looks.

"It ain't half-bad," I said after tasting it with the
soupspoon.

The three made comparisons of the utensil I'd
dipped it out with and tried it. They were hungry, and
that overcame any reservations they had about the
dish.

On the main dish, the new potatoes and peas drew
Erv's words. "They pulled these potatoes too green."
But the girls attacked their steaks with gusto. Stout
wanted the recipe for the French bread, but the waiter
acted dumb. I figured they wanted to keep it a secret.

"I guess we could walk off this meal," I said after
paying us out. I didn't try to use Buster's whorehouse
token, but I did use the rest of his money and some
of mine.

"Next time we better eat at that cowboy café down

by the tracks," Erv said, holding my arm in both hands. "We can eat there for seventy-five cents."

"I guess so. Whoever heard of three dollars apiece for supper?" Tate said, and whistled as she gazed around at the lobby. "They must be getting rich as hell selling food that high."

"Tate!" Erv barked. "Act like a lady."

"At least I ain't hanging all over poor H.B. like he was going to run off and not foot the next bill for our meals."

Erv bolted upright like she had not realized her intimate way of holding my arm so tight. I wished Tate had never told her a thing. I thought I was winning the war—I had Erv off guard and confused. I was doing great.

I had enjoyed her hugging my arm as we crossed the lobby. When we stepped out in the night the girls put up their shawls, and I wished I'd brought my duster to wear over my coat. The stars were out, except for a few clouds. The rain looked like it wasn't coming. Cold as Flagstaff felt, I thought it might snow if it did anything.

A taxi drove up as we stood waiting and deciding which way to go.

"Thank you, Mr. Temple," the cab driver said. I stopped and turned to see the tall man vanish into the lighted lobby. In his expensive high-crowned hat and brown tweed coat, he hardly looked like a ranch manager.

"What's wrong?" Stout asked.

"That's the man heads the Double T ranch."

"So?" Erv asked.

"Somehow the Double T is involved in this rustling and shooting at me," I said, seeing for the first time they had to be.

The girls inhaled sharply.

"Who would ever believe that?" Erv asked.

"That's for me to prove."

❖ 15 ❖

The moment of truth had arrived. We were in the high-ceilinged room on the second floor of the courthouse that housed the sheriff's office. I still wasn't sure I wasn't dreaming.

"H.B., the territory owes you a great debt for eliminating a killer like Buster Kimes," Sheriff Longmont said. "This check can be cashed at the First National Bank for five hundred dollars."

The girls crowded around and looked at the amount penned in on the paper.

"You're some kind of rich, H.B.," Tate said, reaching over to turn the check more in her direction to see.

"My God, Tate," Erv scolded, "you'll have it torn in shreds before he can cash it."

Tate gave her sister a wry look and stepped back.

"Sheriff," I began, wondering how to broach the

subject of the rustling and the big outfit. "I guess you heard about the incident at the hotel last night."

"Yes, I did. Were they pals of Kimes?"

"I kinda figured they were, sir. I first discovered them hiding out in an old homestead shack. They'd been changing brands on cattle, lots of them. But I couldn't hold them by myself, so they got away."

"What did you say they were doing with those cattle?" Longmont looked at me like I was coming from far away. I'd struck a vein; the man was visibly upset.

"Working the brands over. Then I think they were mixing them in with a large herd so they can escape detection."

"Whose?" Longmont demanded. The frown on his face showed his disapproval of my version of the rustling story. There was nothing left for me to do but blurt out my suspicions, though I'd begun to wonder if he was the right one to tell.

"You need to send some of your deputies out to ride through the Double T's herd. I'd stake my wages those blotched brands are among those cattle."

"Double T's?" Longmont scowled at me. "Bentley, that's too farfetched for me to even imagine. Why, those people have more money than the U.S. Treasury. Why would they want to steal cattle? No, I'll tell the brand inspectors to keep an eye peeled. These fall runs, there's lots of cattle coming." The lawman shook his head in disapproval.

He wasn't going to help us. The notion sunk like a knife in my chest. I thanked him, folded my check, put it in my shirt pocket, and buttoned the flap down. We left his office and went down the courthouse stairs.

"Why won't he believe you?" Erv demanded. "He at least should go check that herd."

"I'm not sure. Stout, why don't you watch around back. If I don't miss my guess, in a few minutes Sheriff Longmont is going to rush over to the Cattlemen's Hotel."

"Whatever for?" Erv asked.

"To meet with the ringleader, Mr. Temple, and tell him how I suspect his outfit of the rustling."

"What else can we do?" Erv asked.

"Tate, I want you to go get your horse and ride like blazes for the herd. You tell Mr. Hainey the Double T's changed their plans and are going to bring their cattle in right away. He doesn't have any time to waste."

Stout scowled at me. "How do you know all this?"

"I figure I've just forced their hand. If I'm wrong, then so what? But I think I'm right. Temple learns we're on to him, he's going to hurry up and sell before anything else goes wrong."

"How will they sell the blotched brands?" Stout asked.

"That won't be hard. They'll buy off a brand inspector."

"I'll hurry," Tate said, and left us for the livery. We wished her well, and I figured the matter of getting Hainey on the trail was handled.

"I'll go check on the sheriff," Stout said with a wink. "Where will you two be?"

"First National Bank, collecting my reward," I said, and offered my arm to Erv. She nodded to Stout and, very ladylike, accepted my elbow. We walked in the warm sunshine down the sidewalk.

The cashier in the bank looked shocked when he read the amount on the check, and disappeared. Erv gave me a guessing look about his reaction when the man left us standing in front of the grilled window. I shrugged. The employee returned accompanied by a portly man with a great ivory mustache and gold watch chain.

"Mr. Bentley, sir. I'm Walker Woodson, president of the bank. Would you please come in my office for a moment? It isn't often we have such a celebrity in our bank."

"Yes," I agreed, and motioned Erv to the door.

He unlocked the door to let us in and made a bow with his head and a sweep with his hand. "You must be Mrs. Bentley," he said, but he never saw the peeved look he drew from Erv. He showed each of us to a high-backed leather-upholstered chair facing his desk.

"This is Miss Erv Rice from North Cut. She is a good and dear friend and is accompanying me on this trip," I explained before the *Mrs.* business burned a hole in Erv's hide.

"My pleasure, ma'am. Mr. Bentley, it is very unusual having a man of your obvious valor in my bank collecting such a great reward."

"The check's good?" I asked. Hell, would anything else go wrong?

"Oh, it is fine. Harvard will have the money here in moments. Could I interest you in investing it in something? Stocks, or even banking ventures?"

"No, Miss Rice and I are looking at cattle ranches."

"Oh!" He almost shuddered with excitement at my words. He clasped both his lily-white hands together like he was sure praying for something hard. "Oh, Mr. Bentley, I have some excellent ranches for sale. Could I interest you in looking at them?" If sugar water ever dripped from a man's lips, it did from Woodson's.

"Mr. Woodson, we've had an exhausting trip. I fear Miss Rice is not up to any ranch examinations today, but perhaps we will be later."

"May I send my carriage for you?"

"You just may," I said, and rose. I looked at the pile of money Harvard had placed on the desk. I took Erv's drawstring purse from her, set it on the desk, and put the bundles of bills, one at a time, inside it. My hands were almost shaking. I could hardly believe it was happening. Why, I was rich, by my standards. Finished, I drew the string and handed it to her. "Thanks, sir, and when we get ready to find that special place, we'll be coming around."

"Oh, excellent, Mr. Bentley," he gushed, and we left.

"Why did you tell him that we'd look at his ranches?" she whispered as we went outside the bank.

"I was so dang worried—" I glanced back to be sure no one from the bank could hear me "—he wouldn't pay me otherwise."

I offered her my arm, and she looked at it for a

long moment, then, with a resigned shake of her head, took it. We started back for the courthouse. Stout came hurrying down the street to meet us. When we stopped to wait for her, I saw the ice cream sign and stuck my nose to the window. Sure enough, they had a soda fountain.

"What's in there?" Erv asked, straightening me up.

"What we planned to eat, real ice cream."

Stout gave a "whew" for her short breath. "I ain't sure if he went to the hotel, but the sheriff did leave the courthouse in that direction and in a big hurry. He looked over his shoulder every step."

"You think he's in on it?" Erv asked.

"Well, he could be. This is deeper than I figured. We need to learn all about brand inspectors."

"Why?" Erv asked.

"Because they've got one bought off to work those cattle so the blotched brands go through these yards."

"Why is a rich ranch stealing poor folks' cattle?" Erv asked as I opened the door to the drugstore for them.

"That's beyond me, but it points that folks working inside the Double T are involved, and so are some local lawmen, I figure."

"What are we going to do next?" Stout asked.

"Eat some ice cream and think some more. I wish Mr. Hainey was here—he's good at thinking things out."

Erv clapped my shoulder with her hand. "For a plain old cowboy, H.B., you aren't doing bad." Guess I kinda beamed with that and Stout's nod of approval thrown in, though that didn't help me figure how we'd ever prove the stolen cattle were deep in the Double T herd.

The young man who waited on us brought the half-moons of vanilla-flavored ice cream in little glass dishes on stems, and short silver spoons to eat with. Erv asked me twice under her breath what it cost, but I ignored her. There were a few things in life where you have to say to hell with the costs and on with the pleasure. But she'd learn that hanging around me. I could see Stout was enjoying herself and not begrudging a tasty bite. Erv wasn't doing bad nipping at hers either. I almost forgot about all our troubles as the cold, sweet spoonfuls melted on my tongue and drew up the saliva.

"Are you folks drovers?" the boy asked.

"Yes," I said.

"We get some pretty rowdy cowboys in here sometimes for ice cream," he said. "But you are sure the nice ones."

We thanked him. I could imagine the rowdy ones he meant. Flush full of whiskey that they'd tried to wash the trail dust down with and ready to eat all the ice cream on that mountain above Flag. We finished and I paid the cashier, almost thinking about using the Kimes token. But I didn't want to embarrass the girls.

'Where to next?" Stout asked as we stood in the sunshine.

"The train yards—we've got to reserve pens for the cattle."

"How will you know the crooked brand inspector?" Erv asked.

"I ain't sure, but I've had good luck so far piecing this thing together. Why don't you gals go back to the hotel and wait for me."

"No way!" they said in a chorus. I gave up that notion. I really wanted to ride Short around Flag since my boot soles weren't made for all this walking. Recalling Townsend exiting the cab the night before, I wondered if I should hire a cab to take us.

"I may go see if the horses are all right," I finally mumbled.

"Sure," Erv agreed. They were looking at all the fine houses we passed and the spanking teams and rigs going by. I remembered the taxi, and while I'd never hired one before, I knew they'd haul you for a fee. When the next one came by, I stepped off into the cinder street and stopped him.

"The wagon yard," I said after loading my two companions and seating myself facing them. While they were inspecting the leather luxury and the icing-glass side windows, I was wondering how to handle the situation until Hainey and the others arrived. This bunch might seriously try to remove anyone they thought was in their way.

We arrived at the wagon yard, and I paid the driver the two bits. I left the girls out front and started back. The first thing I noticed was the spotted rump of Tate's paint horse standing beside the gray. What horse had she taken? The gray, her paint, Short, and Stout's horse were all in the tie stall.

I ran to the front as fast as my pointy-toed boots would go. I stopped a whiskered stable hand. "You haven't seen an attractive girl about this tall, fifteen, sixteen or so?"

He shook his head like a wooden Injun. I hurried out front and searched around. "We've got big problems. Tate never made it here."

Erv put her hand to her mouth at the realization. "They've kidnapped her, haven't they? Oh, H.B., we have to do something."

"How did they get her?" Stout set her lips tight looking at me for the answer.

"I don't know, but they aim to use her for our silence. I'd bet a damn whorehouse token on that."

"Why that?" Erv asked with a frown.

"Because I still have Kimes's in my pocket. Come on, I'm going to find the town marshal. I think he may be the only honest one in town."

"What if he isn't?" Stout asked.

"Then I'm getting out my firearms and shooting this whole damn town up until I get some answers. If they hurt a hair on that girl's head, I aim to make them pay."

"Doesn't someone need to go tell Mr. Hainey and the rest?" Erv asked, stopping in her tracks.

"Too dangerous," I said, and dismissed the notion.

"I'm going," Erv said, not moving. "Give me that old pistol of yours. You can buy another one. I can use it if I need to, and I'll be up there to Mormon Lake by dark and have them here in the morning to help you."

"It's a good idea. Erv can ride like an Indian," Stout said.

"Erv, I can't let you go and take a chance on you getting hurt, too."

To my shock, Erv hugged me with a grim set to her oval jaw. Her form pressed hard against me; my breath became short. Then she ripped the Colt out of the back of my waistband. "Buy yourself a good one. You needed a better one than this anyway."

I shook my head as she gathered up her skirts and headed for the livery, her purse hanging from one wrist and the .31 in her right hand. I pitied any outlaw that tried to stop her. Why, they'd read newspapers through him when she got done.

"What now?" Stout asked.

"Take a taxi to the mercantile and buy two pistols. Then I'm finding out who has taken Tate. This is all my fault; I should have gone to tell Hainey myself."

"Tate'll be fine. They ain't stupid enough to hurt her."

"Listen, this deal is a big one for some reason. Anyone in their way is a mere flick of the finger to hard cases like these. If that Longmont is in this, then there's a sheriff and his job at stake. Temple, he's making big wages running that ranch; why would he be involved in stealing cattle?"

"What if none of this is true?" Stout asked, hesitating before she stepped in the taxi.

"Lord, Stout, part of it is. We know that they tried to kill me. Remember those rustlers in the hotel? Still, we have to find Tate. Those rustlers are still on the loose, far as we know."

Stout agreed and took a seat.

At the large mercantile I bought Stout a short-barreled .44. It was large, but it would fit in her purse. I chose a six-inch model and two boxes of shells. The bill came to nearly forty-five dollars, and I counted the money out slowly. I was nearly down to Kimes's token. Erv had my reward money with her!

We left the mercantile, and Stout tried to hand me a few silver dollars.

"You been paying and paying. Here's some money."

I turned her down, but if we took many more taxis or needed our horses, I'd borrow it. "Thanks. If I need it, I'll ask for it."

"Hotel," I told the taxi driver, and we went across town in a clatter of hooves.

The window in the hotel's front door was replaced by plain glass, and the workmen had only just finished when we arrived. They were leaving with their tools when we opened it.

"I'll go check our room," Stout said, and started up the stairs. I strode to the front desk.

"My name's Bentley. Any messages for me?" There was no one in the lobby as I glanced around. My heart sank when the clerk removed an envelope from the cubbyhole and read the name.

"H.B. Bentley?"

"That's me." Stout was already upstairs. I stepped

back from the counter and tore open the envelope.
With weak fingers I opened the one page.

H.B.:
We have the Rice girl. You better ride out of Flag
and take the other women with you. We will release her when our business is over. Stop those
cattle from the North Cut if you want to see her
alive.

I slapped the letter with the back of my free hand.
Why had I wanted to check on those horses?

Either I located this Temple guy and took him hos-
tage in exchange for Tate or I found where they were
holding her. I was beside myself and scratching the
itch on my neck when Marshal McAllen spoke to me.

"Good morning, H.B."

"Morning," I said, taking my hand down. "You
didn't get those two last night, did you?"

"No, they must be hiding under a rug."

"Or someone's hiding them."

"What do you mean?" McAllen looked huffy about
my words.

"Someone—" I guided him aside "—has kidnapped
the youngest Rice girl, Tate. Here's the letter I got."

"When did this happen?" he asked.

"This morning. I sent her to get the North Cut
bunch since I figured that the Double T was moving
their cattle in early."

"Wait, what has this got to do with kidnapping
Tate?"

"Plenty. First, I believe there are stolen cattle in that Double T herd that have blotched brands."

"Why?" The lawman seemed perplexed and very concerned at my every word.

I explained everything leading up to our arrival in Flagstaff, and subsequent happenings, to McAllen. He listened and nodded grimly. "I've suspected Longmont was up to something for a long time. But we're political rivals, so I can't accuse him."

"Then what can we do?"

"Wire the territorial governor. He can send U.S. marshals in to investigate."

"How long will that take?"

"Three, maybe four days."

"Lord, McAllen, they can drive those cattle in and ship them across the country by then, not saying what they'll do to poor Tate."

"Take it easy, Bentley," he said, perturbed with my insistence. "We have to do this by the law. You go up to your room and stay there. I'll put out the word and find where they're holding that girl. I can do that. Someone saw her, and for a price they'll say who has her. You stay upstairs till I get back. I can't have Flagstaff turned into another shoot-'em-up Dodge City."

I agreed to his plan with reservations and met Stout coming down the stairway.

"What's going on?" she said, noticing McAllen going out the front door.

"I've put our fate in his hands. I agreed to stay in my room until he gets back."

"Can we trust him?"

"I have to say, he wasn't surprised about my suspicions of the sheriff or the Double T bringing in those stolen steers. He's going to telegraph the governor for marshals. And then find where they're holding Tate."

"My heavens, H.B., how did we get into such a stir in the first place?" Stout asked.

"Damned if I know." I scratched the itch on my neck and we went up the stairs. Nothing to do but wait. I certainly hoped that Erv was making her way all right to Mormon Lake.

I paced two trails in the hotel room floor. Stout sat on the bed and crossed and recrossed her legs a hundred times. I went out on the veranda and looked across the traffic. A caged mountain lion would have felt easier than I did.

There was a knock on the door, and I cautioned Stout to remain seated. With the new Colt in my hand, I carefully opened the door. McAllen stood there with a mild amount of shock at the pistol pointed at him.

"Sorry," I said, checking the hall to be sure no one was out there. "You learn anything?"

"They're holding her in the White Livestock Commission office down by the stockyards," he said, removing his nice hat and wiping his forehead with his palm. "Two men said they saw a girl by her description being taken there earlier."

"How can we get her out?" I asked, still pacing like a lion. I knew every crack and miscut in the pine flooring.

"Carefully, but we'll have to catch them off guard. We go in there shooting and we may get her killed."

I sobered to that notion. "Wait! What if some crazy-drunk cowboy went on a wild tooter and was raising enough Cain out in the street to distract them, and you slipped in and got her out?"

McAllen blinked his eyes. "A diversion, huh?"

"They'll know you," Stout said.

"Not in the clothes I'm going to wear. I'll get a different hat and some rags from a secondhand store."

"It's too risky for you!" Stout said. "I promised Erv I'd keep you alive till she got back."

"This is for Tate," I said. "Marshal, give me about an hour. I'll throw the damnedest show you ever saw in front of that office. When I do, you just get Tate out."

"I've got two honest deputies; they'll help us."

"Marshal, Stout can shoot with any man, and she's got a big interest in her sister's welfare."

He looked over and nodded his approval. "One thing to remember, Sheriff Longmont has some men on his payroll that might try to interfere for his sake, and I ain't sure how many hands those kidnappers got at White's."

"A chance we'll have to take," I said grimly. We shook hands on it, and he left with Stout in the surrey rig. I headed for the back-street stores where folks traded in old clothes for better used ones.

The short hunchbacked woman who waited on me was toothless. She cackled as well as drooled when she talked.

"Oh, I've got a good four-peak hat right back here," she said, leading me down a dark aisle through piles of sweaty-smelling clothing. Her body odor was ripe, and I was having problems holding down the ice cream.

"There it is," she said proudly, and rammed her fist in it to make the top pop out.

The hat was a dandy. The long coat she found was too big and looked like it had had a wreck with a barbwire fence. The tail was all shredded. An old pair of home-patched high-top boots to tuck my pants in looked good.

She figured for a long time with a stub of a lead pencil, then looked up at me out of her good eye. "Fifty-six cents."

I felt in my pocket and discovered all I had left to pay her with was Kimes's token. I slapped it on the counter.

She looked at it like it was poison.

"Nothing wrong with that token. It's good money anywhere," I said, anxious to be on my way. There was a crowing rooster on one side of the brass coin, the words *Five Dollars* stamped on the other, issued by the Silver Lady Parlor House in Tucson. It was valid currency anywhere on the face of the earth for that amount or an all-nighter.

She looked up and grinned wide at me. "I ain't got change for that."

"Keep it, I'm in a hurry."

"No! No!" she cried, and her talon fingers caught

my sleeve. "I'm an honest businesswoman. I can't take this for only fifty-six cents."

"I've got to run," I said. The clothes, boots, and hat in my arms, I looked down hard at her grip on my arm. Dammit, I needed to be gone. I didn't care if she wondered why I was so damn generous and needed all these fine clothes.

"You come back sometime when you need some real female company and can stay all night with me. I won't even charge you the fifty-six cents you got in clothes," she cackled, and gave a few hee-hees like she'd really enjoy that. "Remember, you got lots of credit with Berthie!"

I nodded and hurried outside, grateful for the fresh air. The sky had clouded over and the air was turning cooler.

By the time I drew Short out of the wagon yard and bought a quart of whiskey on credit to make me smell right, snowflakes were filtering down. I hoped McAllen and Stout hadn't given up on me as I changed clothing in the alleyway. Those crooks would never recognize me in this outfit. The coat smelled like sour puke. I pulled the hat down to my ears, hoping it had been off the former owner long enough that all the head lice had abandoned it.

"Yahoo!" I shouted, coming down the street. I reached back and tickled ol' Short's flank with my spur. He had a kicking fit every time and jolted me around in the saddle as he pumped his heels left and right at everything close. He slammed his shoes into a wagon box and drew an irate shout from a teamster as I closed in on the White Livestock Commission Company. To my left were the railroad and the cattle pens; on the right of the cinder road (fast becoming snow-covered) were various warehouses and livestock commission businesses.

White's name was clearly printed on the false-front building as I whirled Short around and fired the pistol in the air. He kicked up his heels and scattered the horses hitched to the rail. I felt sure they were the rustlers' saddle stock. Reins snapped as the wide-eyed animals shied from his flying hooves.

"Eeh-ha! I'm the wildest puncher that ever left Texas! *Eeh-ha!"* I screamed, and shot another round in the sky. Short was kicking up a storm, and three angry hombres rushed outside in the goose-feather–size snow to see where their horses had gone.

"Stop that, you crazy son of a bitch!" one shouted, and rushed out to take Short's rein and get us away from his horses.

His face went blanched like the big snowflakes when I stuck the gun barrel in his face and whispered, "You're a dead man; tell them to shuck their irons."

"Curly, it's a trap!" he shouted instead.

I clubbed him over the head with the barrel, and to avoid being shot at, I dove off Short's back into a pile with the stricken outlaw. Short was only getting started. He kicked the hitching bar loose, and that pole struck both rustlers in the chest. Knocked back, their shots went wild. I collared the one I had, and Marshal McAllen burst out the front door with a long-barreled pistol.

"She's all right!" he shouted, disarming the other two. "Get your hands up!"

Stout came rushing out with a big smile, and she caught ol' kicking Short by the reins and had him calmed down in a minute.

I shoved my prisoner toward McAllen, who was handcuffing the others. Tate burst out and looked around. In a few short steps, she tackled and hugged the air out of me. Almost in tears, Tate buried her face in the smelly old canvas coat.

"I told them you would come save me!" Tate said.

I smiled at her. Sure glad she had all the faith. I'd worried a lot about it.

"What now?" I asked McAllen as he stood the prisoners up.

"I think these men will be more than willing to tell us the whole story about the rustling. Come on up to my jail; I've got a court reporter ready to take it down."

"Like hell," the bald one said, and spit at our feet.

"Curly," McAllen said, "all you've got is time."

"What about Temple?" I asked.

The lawman gave a disappointed exhalation. "He checked out of the hotel an hour ago and caught the westbound. Sorry, no way I could hold him and not tip these guys off." McAllen shook his head.

I nodded in agreement and then put my arms around the Rice sisters' shoulders. Stout led ol' Short. The North Cut folks were going to recover their cattle. Those U.S. marshals would root out the rest of the operation. Things were turning out better for everyone.

"Really, H.B., where did you get this stinking old torn-up coat? You smell worse than an old dog," Tate said, wrinkling her nose.

"You mean you wouldn't go in the Cattlemen's Hotel restaurant with me in this?"

"H.B. Bentley, I'd ride from hell to breakfast with you." She elbowed me for effect.

"Speaking of that, I sure hope your sister made it to Mormon Lake." I gave a long look to the east, some concerned about her safety.

"She'll be fine. And that's another thing," Stout said as we crossed the double tracks in the heavier snowfall.

"Another thing?" I asked as a large flake fell inside my shirt collar and made me shiver.

"We've decided we don't want you to leave and go back to the Salt River."

"Maybe I can take this reward money and buy me a start."

"Erv's got thirty cows of her own to go in on it with you," Tate said.

"Tate! Dammit, you're rushing this whole thing!" Stout admonished her sister.

Tate ducked and covered her mouth, but I could feel her laughing under her hand.

"Everyone is convinced but Erv," I said as we went inside the wagon yard.

"Future brother-in-law," Stout said, "let me tell you, we can handle her."

Despite the wet snow sticking on my face, I hugged both of them and kissed them on the forehead. Erv didn't know what we had planned for her, but she'd learn quick enough. Ol' Short gave a grunt and kicked his heels up in a flurry of white feathers. My butterfly cowboy days were over.

Adiós, amigos.

About the Author

DUSTY RICHARDS grew up in Arizona and worked ranches there, until his quest to own his own land led him to the Boston Mountains of Arkansas. He is extremely popular in northwest Arkansas as a rodeo announcer, auctioneer, and the man who gives the daily farm report on Channels 29 and 40 in Fayetteville and Springdale. Since 1963 he's been the "chicken doctor" for Tyson Chickens. One of the funniest men around, Dusty has kept his wife, Pat, laughing for over thirty years. He is at work on his next western novel, *By the Cut of Your Clothes*, to be published by Pocket Books.